The
Lehi Tree™

The
Lehi Tree™

Katherine Myers

Green Star
Publishing

Salt Lake City, Utah

ISBN 1-57636-026-1

First Printing, 1996

Printed in the Untied States of America

Special Thanks to:

Vicki Hansen, one of only five people who knows my true writing history (or personal history for that matter) for excellent first and second draft editing; to Pamela Cross for her insights and encouragement; to Linda Callahan, my dearest sister, who has always shared my dreams; and Thank You to the editors at Green Star Publishing for greeting this book with such enthusiasm. But most of all to my husband, Kelly Myers, the most genuine person I know.

And it came to pass that those who tarried with their wives and their children caused that their fair daughters should stand forth and plead with the Lamanites that they would not slay them.

And it came to pass that the Lamanites had compassion on them; for they were charmed with the beauty of their women.

Mosiah 19:13-14

SM

PROLOGUE

L eave the weak ones!" King Noah screamed to his men. "Leave them, or we all die!"*

His face quivering with fear, the king glanced down at the people far below him. Without the vestige of his crimson robe and armor he appeared suddenly awkward, trying to maneuver his heavy girth up the steep hillside. As he peered across the upturned faces that pleaded with him to save them, sweat ran down his cheeks, glistening on his black beard. Looking further down the hill, he saw cimeters raised, the black swords slicing downwards, the screams of his dying soldiers traveling on the wind. Hysteria ran like a wave through the people, arrows suddenly piercing the throng.

In desperation many looked to their ruler. Did he not have the wisdom to save them? Some of his people reached out in pleading, calling his name.

"Leave them!" he screamed again, his voice high-pitched with fear.

"No!" one man cried in protest. Yet even as he spoke, the words stilled on his lips. He sank to the ground, an arrow deep within his heart.

Many of the men turned to flee as King Noah showed them how simple a task it was to sacrifice others for one's self. He clawed his way up the hillside, his meaty fists grabbing at the bushes as he heaved his frame towards the top. The action caused his crown to fall from his head, and it rolled down the hill. Heedless, he hurried on.

* Mosiah 19:9-12

Screams of terror and war cries echoed against the hill-side as the people tried to follow their king and his men across the rocky climb. Yet there were too many women and infants, too many old men and children to outrace the warriors who pursued them. And after so many battles, there were not enough fighters left to hold off the venge-ful foe that closed in on them. Sensing their imminent death, the people knew there would be no escape. Terri-fied mothers clutched their sobbing infants and scrambled over rocks and loose shale. Fathers grabbed their ex-hausted children, dragging them ever upwards.

Some of the men, bent on saving their families, turned and drew their weapons, knowing that they sacrificed their lives so that their loved ones might live a moment longer.

It wasn't so with the king's priests. Without hesita-tion they scrambled across the hill after their king, not a selfless emotion left in them. Nevertheless, there was one, the priest named Cumeni, who instinctively paused to look down the hill. He could see, far below, his daughter Kheronai. She looked up at him, her eyes strangely calm amid the madness. He felt a pang of uneasiness, but he had for too long now followed his king. He turned and fled across the top of the hill.

Overhead the sky had darkened. Thick gray clouds lay like weaver's wool upon the expanse, allowing only a dim light to filter through. A few drops of rain began to fall. As Kheronai watched her father turn from her, her heart thudded like a slow death dirge within her chest. Feeling a trembling hand on her arm, she looked into the face of Riplah, her mother's father.

"Riplah!" she choked. "What must we do?"

Below them, at the base of the hill, the Lamanite slaughter continued unabated. Riplah's ancient frame was weak, but his voice was steady. "My fair daughter, you must plead with the Lamanites for our lives." Then, turning to the throng, he cried, "Listen! Our daughters must plead for us!"

Kheronai stared at the man who after her mother's death had raised her. Would he elect to hasten her death? The terror that clawed at her was almost more than she could bear, but she lifted eyes of trust to him.

"Yes!" another shouted. He grabbed his daughter's arm. "Go down! Plead for our lives lest they destroy all of our race!"

The girl nearly crumpled. "They will slay me!" she wailed.

The father struck her and she staggered back, her sobbing sisters reaching out to her. Other fathers grabbed their daughters as if to shove them down the hill. Kheronai turned to them.

"Why do you weep? Shall we not die, even this day? Let us plead for the lives of our families, that they might take pity on us and perhaps spare our people. I will go," she said. She turned and walked down the hill. She was soon followed by the other young women, some pushed by their fathers, others joining Kheronai of their own will.

The way down the hill was swift and they neared the base where many of their brothers and fathers lay in death. They heard the moans of the dying and smelled the stink of death and blood. The Lamanite warriors were terrible in their destruction, their cimeters and lances stained crimson.

A deep roll of thunder echoed across the valley of Nephi and reverberated against the hills. The soldiers moved forward, cries of victory on their lips, the last of the Nephite warriors falling beneath their swords. Suddenly the Lamanite soldier in the lead paused as a Nephite maiden ran forward and sank to her knees, her arms out, her palms turned upwards in a plea for mercy. The

Lamanite leader was heavily muscled, his black hair caught back with a twisted band. His face was stern and his body splattered with the blood of many Nephites. Clad in breech cloth and leggings, he held his cimeter high over his head. The day's light glinted dully off its stained surface and the copper wristbands he wore.

Never had Kheronai known such fear. Never had she imagined such a terrifying image of death. She knelt before the fearsome warrior and turned her eyes pleadingly toward him, despite the huge curved weapon with its blades of black obsidian poised to slice into her. His dark eyes studied her, his impassive face appearing to be carved of stone. The cimeter's slight movement gave her certain knowledge that in a moment the death blow would come.

The weight of the heavy cimeter strained the muscles in Zeram's arms, yet he froze as he stared at the vision before him. His head pounded and his chest heaved as he gasped for air. Never had he fought so noble a battle against his hated foe, but now he felt uncertain with what he saw before him. At his feet knelt a maiden whose fair face looked up at him beseechingly. Her arms were stretched out toward him, her palms turned upwards in a plea for mercy. Her hair fell unbound, flowing like dark honey away from an exquisitely lovely face. Brown eyes, a lighter hue than his own, gazed up at his, and her countenance was strangely calm as she awaited his decision. Behind her, the other maidens had knelt, looking up at his brethren with tearful faces. His eyes regarded the maiden who knelt directly before him. Grief etched her beautiful features, but there were no tears. He lowered his weapon.

Kheronai gasped, for a moment not believing her enemy's sudden act of mercy. But she had only an instant to wonder at this miracle, for a war cry pierced the air and another warrior ran forward, his lance directed to her heart. The first

Lamanite quickly bolted forward and seized the murderous weapon, running it into the ground where it snapped in half. At his sharp command, the other warriors lowered their weapons as well, looking at the fair Nephite maidens who pleaded for their lives, and those of their families. Charmed by their beauty, they felt a strange compassion for the children of their enemy, and their thirst for blood subsided.

A cry escaped Kheronai as Zeram, the Lamanite leader, reached down and pulled her to her feet. He studied her face impassively, then released her and she stumbled backward. "Your cries for mercy have been heard," he said at last.

From out of the hills came groups of people led by the Lamanites. Where once they had scrambled upwards to escape, now they miserably plodded back down the hill. None could fathom what would happen to them now that they had fallen prey to their fiercest adversary. All they knew was that they had been spared from the sword. Mothers hushed their crying children while men carried down the wounded. A light rain began to fall with soft plopping sounds as moans from the injured pierced the air.

The rain fell like ice on Zeram's heated chest and face. His thirst for war satisfied, he motioned to several Nephite men to gather wood. With the aid of seedpods and brush, they struck flint and the kindling started to burn. After the first fire was built, several others were made, giving warmth to those who huddled near.

Standing in the rain, Kheronai shivered slightly. She knew that rather than the chill air of the storm, it was the aftermath of her ordeal that caused her body to shudder. She wrapped her arms about herself, glancing for a moment at the Lamanite warrior who had spared her as he stood silently watching his people take hers captive. The fear that had led her to kneel before him and plead for mercy now left her numb. All about her stood terrible destruction, and nothing but a promise of bondage.

Kheronai searched the crowds of defeated people for her beloved grandfather. At last she spied him in the arms of Gideon, the Nephite captain, and she hurried towards them. "Riplah," she cried wretchedly, reaching out to her grandfather.

The old man turned his head to her. The broken shaft of an arrow in his bony chest made each breath a struggle. His voice labored to reach her. "Kheronai, beloved! Child of my child. . . ." He closed his eyes against the pain.

She watched the rain mingle with the blood on his chest, the dark stain so frighteningly foreign to her. "Gideon!" she whispered in anguish to the soldier who laid the dying man beside the fire to ease his final moments. "How can this have happened to us?" she said, forcing back the sobs that made her throat ache for release, as Gideon offered her his cloak to cover Riplah.

Gideon seethed with rage. "I should have slain that wretched Noah, who dared call himself sire of our land, while I had the chance. My sword was drawn to do so when he climbed the tower to escape. When he saw the approach of the soldiers, he pleaded our people's cause and begged me to spare him, but he cared only enough to save himself!* He thought nothing of his people and has shown us that much this very day. Did not the mighty King Noah and his priests leave us as prey to our foe?"

"And among them, my father," she whispered, the memory stinging her very soul.

Gideon's rage softened at the grief in Kheronai's voice.

* Mosiah 19:4-8

"Cumeni fled, then?" She nodded and his scowl deepened. "How bitter is this day, when children are cast aside by their fathers who would only save themselves!"

Kheronai could not answer. Instead she knelt beside Riplah, her head bent over him, tears mingling with the rain on her face. Gideon stood helpless at the death of his old friend and at the pain of his friend's beloved grandchild. He stroked Kheronai's hair wordlessly, then turned away to see where else help was needed among his people.

Lost in grief, Kheronai didn't notice when the rain ceased and night descended on the valley. Instead she sat quietly, Riplah's head in her lap as she gently stroked his wrinkled face and the feathery tufts of white hair. Although she knew his end was near, she prayed for him to live. He was all she had, now that her father had deserted her. At the thought of his abandonment, Kheronai's heart grew more and more bitter.

Cumeni had been a statesman and priest, honored and respected by many. Although she had never known the comfortable ease with him that she had with Riplah, still she had loved him. In the glow of the fire, she bitterly reflected how he had traded that love for his own safety, willingly sacrificing herself and Riplah to save his life. Because of his cowardice her dearest teacher and friend now lay dying.

When at last Riplah opened his eyes, he became aware of the warm flicker of firelight, of a black sky that had cleared to let him see the stars. He stared up at a strangely bright star overhead, feeling that his very soul was being pulled towards that point of light.

"Grandfather," Kheronai said tenderly, her fingers gently stroking his wrinkled face.

"Kheronai," he murmured weakly. "Daughter of my

daughter. . . . You are much like Lia, your mother. In her death it was you who became the child of my old age."

"The Lamanite soldiers have spared us," she said quietly.

"I knew it would be so," he replied. "Yet you did not. You went down to die, my daughter, and now your people live, because of it." He fell thoughtful for a moment. "Are we captives of the Lamanites, then?"

"Yes, Grandfather."

He tried to speak, but began to choke and it was some time before he could find his voice. "Tell me what you will do, when I am gone."

Tears stung her eyes. "I do not know. Cumeni has deserted us. He followed King Noah." She bitterly answered.

"Cumeni deserted you long ago, when he turned to the priestcrafts of Noah." The old man sighed. "Still, it was not always so when Lia was yet alive. There was a gentle spirit in your mother and her beauty was born of kindness. She influenced others for good, including your father. Yet when she died, so did the good that was in Cumeni. Now, with the coming of wickedness, and the murder of the Prophet Abinadi, the very city of Nephi has crumbled."*

"What will become of us?" Kheronai asked wretchedly.

"You must seek Alma," Riplah answered, his voice gaining strength for the first time. His words startled her.

"Do you speak of the priest who served with my father, he who King Noah sought to slay?" the words trembled on her lips. How angry her father had been when he spoke of Abinadi who had rebuked the king and his high priests! No man should be allowed to speak that way of his king and religious leaders, and live. How could the young priest Alma be so foolish as to support the man's teachings? Cumeni had raged.

"The same!" Riplah grasped Kheronai's hand with a

* Mosiah 17:9-20

strange force. "He and his people have fled, and you must find them."

"Why should I do this?" she questioned uncertainly.

"Alma is a righteous man, a man who knew of God. You remember the things I have taught you, and counseled you to keep secret from your father?" He paused and she nodded. "It was Alma who instructed me of such," Riplah continued, "and I would have fled with him save for the daughter of my old age. I could not persuade Cumeni to seek the light, yet neither could I abandon you."

"And now my father has abandoned me," she answered bitterly.

Riplah struggled with each breath he took. "Swear an oath!" he rasped out. Weakly he caught her hand, placing it beneath his thigh. "Swear that you will leave the land of Nephi, and travel to the Waters of Mormon. It is last where Alma and his people were known. The Lord God of Israel will guide you."

He shook while he held her hand, his efforts taking the last thread of his strength. "I swear it," she said.

The words had barely been spoken when his body went limp, her oath setting him free. Kheronai touched his face.

"Dear Grandfather," she whispered, although she knew he had left her. When he made no response, she slid her hand across his eyelids, then bent her head and wept. Despair overcame her and she lifted her voice in a loud wail. Her weeping could not be stilled, nor would the pain in her chest cease.

Standing apart from the captives, Zeram watched as the pale smoke wafted upward against the black sky. He heard the Nephite maiden lift her loud mourning trill to the sky and he saw other women join her, their strange cries echoing together in the night.

He watched as Kheronai walked to the fire and knelt down beside it. She grabbed the neck of her silk tunic, rending it, then reached into the edge of the coals, filling her palms with ash and pouring it over her head. Her body rocked back and forth in mourning, her keening melding with the voices of the others.

Two women knelt beside her, their own faces streaked with tears.

"Kheronai, what comfort can be given in this day of our misery?"

"Indeed, Kheronai. What comfort can be given?" the second echoed.

Slowly she lifted up her face, peering at the stars overhead for a while. When she finally turned to look at the two women, her countenance appeared to be made of stone. "Do not call me Kheronai," she said harshly. "That will be my name no more, forever. This day I shall be called Mara, for my soul is bitter. I have seen my own father turn from me, even as I have seen the king of our people turn from us all. They left us to be destroyed, and now because of this we are taken into bondage. I have knelt before my enemy to plead for mercy, this day, and have seen the father of my mother killed. There is no joy in me. I am Mara."

The other women stared at her in astonishment. They didn't know what to say to the young maiden who had saved their lives, but then had changed her name to mean bitterness. The two women withdrew awkwardly as Mara pulled back her hair and twisted it into a straight cord over her shoulder. Then she took her grandfather's knife in her free hand to cut off her hair, the final sign of mourning.

Suddenly her hand was jerked upwards, a blow knocking the knife into the fire where it lay on the coals. With a cry she stared up at the large Lamanite warrior who towered over her. The misery of her mourning vanished as fear bit into her and she clutched her throbbing wrist. In the flickering light of the fire, Zeram's features took on the appearance of chiseled amber. His black eyes pierced her, somber and disapproving, and she felt confused, not knowing if his actions forbade her to mourn or to possess the knife. Slowly she lowered her head and felt, rather than saw him, turn and walk away, choosing a seat on the ground not far from her place by the fire. She felt his eyes upon her, slicing through her like a sharp-edged cimeter.

The night air grew cold and still, the fires burning low as exhausted children slept while their parents lay on the ground, unable to ease their fatigue. All about them Lamanite guards moved, restlessly watching their captives. Mara lay down, resting her head on her arms. From where she lay, she could see the Lamanite warrior, could feel his eyes continually on her. In the shadows she couldn't see the direction of his gaze, but sensed the way it held her prisoner.

Despite the damp ground, the coals of the fire warmed her back, and she felt like sobbing with misery. Yet she had no strength left to cry. Instead she closed her stinging eyes, thinking of her oath to Riplah.

The memory of it gave her sudden hope and she renewed the vow in her heart. She would watch and wait until the time was right. Then she would escape the Lamanite captivity, escape the bitter memories of this day in the valley of Nephi, and find the man named Alma.

CHAPTER ONE

The dream wove itself about Mara, silken cords that began to grow painful, tightening like the encircling grip of a snake. Snatches of memory stung her, biting with the pain that had no balm. With a gasp she awoke, her heart racing within her chest. She forced herself to lie calm, looking about the dim interior of her chamber until reality returned.

Mara took in slow breaths, waiting for the dream to fade as the forest mists did under the warmth of the morning sun. The tightness in her chest finally eased, and she wondered how a mere dream could still have such power over her. The dream seldom differed, playing out the macabre memory of the day her people were taken captive by the Lamanites.

It began with her racing up the hill, never quite able to reach the top where her father stood. No matter how she struggled and called his name, still he left her behind. Slowly she would turn to face the foe who stood like a giant, his huge sword poised above her.

Sometimes the dream ended there, with her jerking awake. Sometimes it continued on, as she helplessly clutched her beloved grandfather to her, begging him not to leave her. Yet this time there had been something more, something that haunted her still.

Mara sat up on the flat pallet, pulling her knees in and resting her head on her arms. What had been different this time? Suddenly she lifted her face, staring down at her palm. In the dream she had felt Riplah's ancient fingers clutch her hand, placing it beneath his thigh in the oath she made. That was the difference! She had almost forgotten her oath to Grandfather.

Mara rose wearily, shivering slightly despite the stuffy air in her chamber. How long had it been? She counted the seasons, realizing over two years had passed. And yet still the dream came, filling her with the same fear and misery which she had felt that very day.

She walked to a large clay ewer, seating herself on the stool beside it and washed her face and hands with the warm water. She dried her face on the hem of her shift, then paused, her mind voicing the thoughts her lips would not say. In all things she had honored the will of her grandfather, yet in his last request she had failed him. An oath had been made at his death, and yet two years had passed away leaving the promise unfulfilled.

"Yet how can I keep this promise?" she wondered unhappily. "Our foes guard the borders of our land so that none can escape. A few have tried, and each of those have felt the bite of the Lamanite sword. What chance have I, a mere woman, when men of great strength have failed?"

Mara shook her head, the rationalization of her words having the bitter taste of cowardice. In the beginning she had schemed, plotting to escape. Yet with each death of those who tried to flee, and the tightening of the forces of the Lamanites, her cause had lost its strength. Hopelessness bound her more tightly in her wretched situation than any chains could.

Still, she faced the truth she had been avoiding. She must keep the promise! To her people an oath stood above all else in importance, and this one seemed even more sacred, sworn at the death of one she loved. "Oh, Grandfather," she cried, suddenly missing Riplah with an intensity she had not felt for some while, "I want to honor my vow to you. It is not that I break it, only that it is left unfulfilled."

A sliver of rose-hued light lined the edge of the window sill of the single high window. It caught Mara's attention, pulling her from her reverie, and she stood quietly. Then she took up her ragged brown tunic, and slipping off her shift, she dressed quickly. She knew she had no more time for melancholy thoughts. Hastily she knotted the sash low about her waist, and slid her feet into worn sandals. She ran her fingers through her tangled hair and smoothed the worn linen tunic she wore. The last clothing left to her, it was only a remnant of a time now gone.

Once Mara had worn the finest tunics of purple and blue linen, yet now she wore the rough cloth of the poor. Gold hoops had once hung from her ears and adorned her wrists; now her arms were bare. Others had combed and perfumed her hair, whereas now she struggled with the tangled mass herself. Her palms had been soft then, doing nothing more difficult than strumming a lute. Now they were rough and stained with potter's clay.

She pulled the long head cloth over her hair and secured it in place with a twisted band of linen. Then snatching up a maize cake and sliding it in her pocket to eat later, she hurried from the tiny, circular chamber. Her room was one of many along the east wall of the city, a small dwelling where she slept at night. It was all she could afford, paying from the few coins she earned. The fine, high towers in which her family had lived were far across the city. She never went there now.

Out in the cool morning air, Mara took a deep breath, trying to clear her head. Her feet flew down the familiar, twisted causeways of the city, hurrying over low stone steps and along narrow lanes. Morning light shone over the stones of the city wall by the time she reached the open market-place. Already wares were being set out by other merchants when she arrived at the small potter's stand. Immediately she began taking out the glazed ewers and bowls for display, but not before Mahijah saw her.

He said nothing, scowling in a silence that invited no explanation. Mara lowered her eyes, busying herself with setting out the pottery to display as Mahijah stood glaring at her. A large man with a black beard and thick arms, his disposition fit his forbidding appearance. Finally he turned and went back through the open doorway and Mara sighed. A moment later a young boy slipped outside, glancing over his shoulder.

"Mara," he spoke in a whisper. "What have you done to make father angry?"

"I only just came, Oriah," she replied in a low voice.

"Ah," Oriah said knowingly, "he does not like it when you are not here before sunrise." As Mara's countenance paled, he consoled her, "Still, what can he do? You paint the finest designs of any pottery merchant in the city."

Mara smiled at him, setting the last of the sculptured jugs on the top shelf. Then she quickly drew out her paint pots and filled a wooden water bowl. A few moments later an old man joined her at the open air table where she sat, and Mara pulled out his stool with a loud thump so he could find it.

"Good morrow, Benjamin," Mara said, but Benjamin made no reply as he felt for the table and stool, and seated himself. Reaching into the vat beside him, he scooped up the thick clay and slapped it onto the table, his gnarled fingers magically working the material.

Despite having grown used to the sight, Mara still marveled at how he could shape the clay pots and ewers. His eyes had grown so dim with age that he relied on Mara or others to tell him the happenings in the marketplace. Yet his fingers were not blind, for when they felt the clay they played out the shapes in his mind. He molded beautiful pots and bowls, designed in the shape of a warrior, a fish, or perhaps a jaguar. As he worked, his fingers continually dipped into a bowl of water, smoothing and shaping the clay.

"So," Benjamin spoke at last. "You were late this morning, Mara. Mahijah is not happy." Mara grimaced, and as though he could see the expression on her face, he chuckled and continued. "He would like to find a reason to be rid of you. That day will come, too. Young Oriah gets better with the paints every day, and soon he will be skilled enough to take over all the painting."

"Yes, Father," she said, using the term of respect which she had adopted for this kindly older man. She knew he was right. Mahijah had only allowed her to come and help in the beginning because his father, Benjamin, had insisted. Benjamin had been a friend to Riplah, and when he learned that others had moved into Mara's home, while she gleaned the fields to survive, Benjamin insisted that she come work with his family selling pottery. Mahijah had honored his father's request, partly because he had been on the hill the day she led the maidens down to plead for her people's cause. But time had dimmed that memory and now he almost resented her for the fine skill she bore with the stylus and dye.

Mahijah's hands were too large to sculpt the pottery, and he didn't have the skill of painting. Instead he glazed and heated the pottery in the stone ovens, while his oldest son Neum learned sculpting from Benjamin. When Mara first tried her hand with painting the crockery, Mahijah had not wanted to admit her skill, but he grudgingly allowed her to paint the pots because she seemed to have a natural ability to color the pottery in a way that enhanced his father's designs. Yet for the last two seasons he had urged Oriah more and more to take up the stylus and paints.

"When I go the way of all the earth, who will watch over you, Mara?" Benjamin asked, almost seeming to perceive her thoughts. "Mahijah will send you away, and no other potter will give you hire. Because you are a woman your skill will stand as naught. It is time you found a husband."

She had heard this refrain often, but suddenly it filled her with a despair that turned to anger. "And how shall I find a husband? Many of those whom I might have chosen died on the hill fighting our enemy. There are almost no men left in our city."

Benjamin grew thoughtful, his hands pausing in the work. "This is so. But still, there are some. . . ."

"Who would choose one such as I?" she said. "I am not the maiden of my father's house. My skin no longer smells of fine oils and spikenard—instead I carry the scent of clay. My robes are coarse and soiled, not fine-twined like those I once wore. Our people are a captive people, and I bear the wretchedness of knowing what we once were, and what we have now become."

She picked up the stylus to which several strands of goat's hair were tied, and dipping it in the yellow ochre drew a fine line of color around the edge of a bowl. At her words, Benjamin was silent and his hands resumed his work. Mara had never spoken to him in such a manner before, and he felt her words.

"Oriah tells me you are beautiful," he said in a gruff manner.

Mara's heart grew tender. Benjamin seldom admitted how dim his sight had grown. "Oriah is only a child," she said quietly.

During the hours that followed, Mara lost herself in her

work. Green-blue, purple, white, and garnet-red brought the shape of the plumed bird to life. She paused only once to eat her small cake of ground corn, putting all her attention on the piece of pottery. As she added the last strokes of yellow, she smiled in satisfaction and stretched, allowing her eyes to wander across the busy marketplace.

Merchants bartered and sold their wares with age-old chants, but beneath the surface there seemed to be a strain of tension. The faces of those who worked showed the desperation to provide for the same needs with half as much because their captors now took half of all they made.* Although the people put on a brave display, the truth manifested itself more clearly than ever to Mara. She saw it in the anxious plea to buy, the envious looks when another merchant made a coin, the laughter grown too harsh.

The sun stood overhead when Naamah, Mahijah's wife, served the noonday meal. In accordance with the family custom, everyone ate inside the dwelling except for Mara who stayed to watch the pottery. Naamah brought her a bowl of goat's meat, bread, and cheese curds, then returned to oversee her family. Mara didn't mind eating alone. There was no place for her with Benjamin's kin, and she felt more comfortable away from Mahijah's stern glances.

As she ate, her mind returned to her night's dream and for the first time in many seasons, she thought about the teachings of Riplah. His lessons now seemed in such contrast to what she lived day by day. He had spoken of the goodness of God, the need to be kind to one another, of hope, but now hardship and unkindness had become her lot.

In the beginning she hadn't truly understood Riplah's dying request. She had only thought he wanted her to find the high priest Alma and his people so that she might finish the lessons he had begun. Yet now, looking at the hardness

* Mosiah 7:15; 19:22

of her own people and remembering the kind teachings of her wise teacher, the contrast struck her. Mara suddenly realized that the bitterness of her situation came from more than the captivity of her city. A hardness of soul had overtaken her people, and she longed more than anything for the words and deeds of kindness she had known from her grandfather. If the people of Alma believed as Riplah did, wouldn't they have the kindness in their hearts that had disappeared from the land of Lehi-Nephi?

Mara felt an overwhelming longing for what had been missing from her life. If she could find the people who believed in the same God as Riplah had, she might regain the happiness once known. Hope began to lighten her heart, but died abruptly as she thought of the people of Alma and where they might be. Could she find the place Riplah had spoken of? Did she remember his directions and had he told her enough to find the way? Then another thought began to crush her hope. What if she traveled through the wilderness to the place where Riplah said they would be, and they had moved on? So much time had passed since his death, and there was no certainty the people still remained at the place Riplah had called the Waters of Mormon.

Despair filled her and suddenly she stood, as if to flee her prison. Quickly she made her way through the marketplace, greeting without thought those who spoke to her. Soon she reached her destination and sat at the edge of the large stone well to draw water. Peering down into the blackened depths of the hole, she again felt the hopelessness of her quest. How could she do the thing which Riplah had asked? As her eyes studied the darkened depths beneath her, a calmness came to her mind, a memory so clear that she felt as if she were once again sitting on a pillow at her grandfather's feet, hearing his kindly voice.

"How shall it be, Grandfather?" her voice seemed to echo from the past.

Riplah had smiled lovingly and stroked her hair. "It shall be, because with the God of Abraham and of Isaac and of Jacob and of all our holy fathers, any such thing is possible. Whatsoever we desire, in righteousness, will be given to us if we only do the will of the Father."

The clear memory was but a brief segment out of time, like a small piece of fabric sheared from a length of cloth. She could not recall the moments before or after, yet his words rang clear to her mind. He had taught her such things, and no matter that so much time had passed, or that her captivity made the promise appear too difficult to keep, Riplah's words were even more true in memory than on the day he had spoken them.

Mara dipped a small gourd into the ewer she had drawn, drinking the cold water to refresh her against the growing heat of day. She slowly returned to the potter's stall, feeling more at peace each time she remembered his words.

It was near the end of the day when Mara saw him. She had just painted the intricate lines of a clay jug in the shape of a puma's head, and the last of the white glaze on the barred teeth of the animal. Setting it down, she studied it with a critical eye. This favorite pot of Benjamin's sold well and she painted it often. Once heated to set the glaze it would look like the one on the shelf.

Young Oriah sat beside her, carefully glazing a jug with goat horn handles. As Mara watched him work, she complemented him. "You grow more skilled each day."

He smiled. "Tomorrow Father says I may try a lion," he said, nodding at the pottery she worked on.

She inclined her head but said nothing. Benjamin had been right. Every day Mahijah urged his son to do more.

Soon there would be nothing left that Oriah couldn't paint with skill, and then there would be no place for her at the potter's stall.

Mara, preoccupied with the thoughts that had followed her through the day, began to finish the last trim of gold paint on the pottery. So involved was she in her work that she didn't notice the sudden silence in the marketplace and the sound of heavy feet. Nor did she see the warriors enter the marketplace until Benjamin touched her with his hand.

"Lamanites?" he questioned in a low voice.

Mara looked up and grew tense beneath his touch. It was answer enough for the old potter. "How many?" he asked.

She quickly counted the backs that passed. "Ten and three."

"Most of them stand at the food places," Oriah added in a low voice. "They look fierce. Some of them have shaved heads."

Benjamin nodded, his ears straining to take in the scene his dim vision couldn't. Mara lowered her head, focusing her attention on the ewer. It wasn't uncommon for the guards who took tribute to pass through the open market, and because they were the task masters they could take whatever things they desired.

Mara did not look up, hoping they would pass by the potter's shop. In the past they had taken little pottery, their interests falling instead upon the sellers of cloth and tools, food and works of fine ore. The fear she felt at seeing them, the fear of that terrible day on the hill, began to loosen its hold upon her as she sensed them moving further down the row of open stalls. Then a shadow fell across her, and involuntarily she lifted startled eyes.

A gasp caught in her throat. Before her stood the Lamanite warrior of that dreadful day. He appeared no different than he had two years before—and no different than he had in her dreams. Behind him the slanting rays of afternoon sunlight edged his form with a thread of gold and made the shadow he cast across her all the more ominous.

His black hair and bronze skin were similar to that of his companions, although he stood slightly taller and wore a light cloak. His dark eyes and the handsome strength of his face held Mara captive until she willed herself to lower her trembling gaze.

She forced herself to sit calmly beneath his deliberate stare. For a moment she thought that perhaps he wouldn't recognize her from that long ago day, that he was only surveying their wares. But when he remained motionless, she knew he was watching her for some sign. When she forced herself to look up, he was not looking at her pottery, but at her.

As she gazed up at him, she pushed back the fear that threatened, meeting his eyes defiantly. His dark gaze didn't waver as he studied her face. When he finally looked away, it was to point to a piece of pottery on the shelf. Oriah jumped up from his stool, and taking the clay pot from the shelf, held it out to the Lamanite soldier.

Mara observed that the ewer he took was a replica of the exact piece she worked on. Watching him take the pottery from Oriah's hands, his gaze still on her, she didn't know what to think. The Lamanite warrior took a flat ring of silver from a wooden rod on his belt, and tossed a shiblon on the table where it clattered in a circular motion before falling still. With a swift turn he left to rejoin his companions, and Mara watched his cloaked back disappear into the crowd.

"What is it?" old Benjamin asked.

"A Lamanite soldier stopped and took one of our pots," Oriah said. "The one of the snarling lion that you made and Mara painted."

The potter and his wife hurried into the stall. "A silver

shiblon!" Naamah said in a harsh whisper, picking up the coin and examining it. She handed it to her husband. "He took the lion ewer and left payment!"

"Why did he give coin?" Mahijah asked. "He could have taken the pot. In truth he could have taken half of all the pots here, and we would not have been able to speak a word. But instead he gave a shiblon for it, when it is hardly worth a leah, or at most, a shiblum."

"Perhaps the soldier liked Mara's work, Father," Oriah said. "He looked at her in a most strange manner before he took it."

"Yes, I saw," Mahijah said, and Mara knew that both he and Naamah had watched the scene from the doorway. "There is no good cause in this thing," he finally stated. "None of their kind has ever given payment before. I fear he wishes to buy something other than a mere piece of pottery."

Mahijah's words stung Mara and she felt the eyes of the others studying her. She was silent as she rinsed out her stylus and covered the paint pots. When the table was in order she said quietly, "I have finished the last piece given me. May I take leave?"

The potter studied her for a moment, then lifted his hand in dismissal. Mara bowed her head and left the shop, hurrying from the market. Once out of the crowded square and away from the din of voices, she felt less turmoil, though her heart was still racing. Weaving her way down the twisted causeway of the city she eventually found herself in a place of very few people, a small open courtyard on the outer edge of the city. In the distance, far across the city, she could see the high, sloping tower of the king's palace and next to it the gleaming stones of the temple.

Pausing in the courtyard Mara looked around uncertainly, not knowing where to go because of the thoughts which trapped her. The turmoil within made her feel confused and uncertain. Why had the Lamanite soldier acted in such a manner? Did he see that she was the same maiden who had knelt before him in the heat of battle, pleading for her life and those of the others?

She tried to calm herself, wanting to believe that he didn't know who she was, that he didn't remember her. There were many maidens that day, many who knelt and pleaded with their foe. And yet she clearly remembered him, didn't she? Many enemy warriors had come to the market, and many had passed by the potter's place. And although they had frightened her with their fierce appearances, none had struck her as this one had.

Even if he did remember her from the first day of the Nephite captivity, what could she mean to him now? "I am nothing more than a maiden who sells pots of clay," she told herself, seeking reassurance. Still, she could not forget his impassive gaze and the quick motion of his fingers which sent the piece of silver clattering onto the table. Despite the warmth of the early evening breeze, Mara shuddered and pulled her head shawl about her.

Mara neared the edge of an enclosed pool of water, staring down into the clear water which magnified the size of the stones. The pool was formed from one of the stone viaducts that passed beneath the outer wall into the city. She took in a slow breath, trying to make her heart slow its quickened pace. The strangeness of the day and its happenings made her grow somber. First the dream, and now this! "I must honor the vow," she said to herself. "What else can it all mean? If the warrior who haunts my dreams now appears in the hours of the day, then the time has come for me to flee. I will leave this city and do as Grandfather requested, if only God will show me the way!"

Mara knew there must be some way to leave the city, some place through which she could escape. But the portals in the walls were narrow and guarded, the windows in the ground dwellings too small for even a child to pass through. She sighed, scooping her hand into the pool and letting the water stream through her fingers. A slow, growing awareness flickered in her mind and she lowered her hand, staring at the channel of water. Sudden excitement flooded her veins.

This was the way! She stood, her eyes fixed on the pool of water and the viaduct from which it had come. Water flowed into the city, filling pools and fountains through the stone channels' deep entryways. She stared at the low arch of the thick city wall, her mind playing out the possibilities. It would be difficult with the swiftness of the water and no airspace beneath the arch, but perhaps if she planned well and moved quickly. . . .

Mara paused, thinking of the Lamanite guards who bordered the land. She forced the discouraging knowledge from her mind. If there was a way out of the city, then there would be a way out of the land. The soldiers looked for groups of Nephite men, not a lone maiden who might be able to slip through the fields at night and into the forest.

Mara's mind pursued the scheme, so engrossed in her thoughts that she didn't see the Lamanite warrior enter the courtyard.

CHAPTER TWO

The Lamanite soldier walked with his companions, who discussed some of what they saw in the market. Yet Zeram was quiet, not wishing to join in the conversation. He was weary from the mission his king had sent him on. The dwelling place of the Nephites felt strange to him and he decided to leave on the morrow after speaking with the overseer of the tribute. Anxiously he thought of returning home to the land of Shemlon where he could see the faces of friends and family, and most especially that of his sister Saphira. He smiled, thinking of the maiden whose gentle ways appealed to all.

His sister had always been quicker to laughter than he, with a more playful and forgiving nature. Saphira's ways were a pleasure to be near, and she was a hard worker, too. She kept his dwelling in order and his food always hot. Yet it was not only her pleasant ways that drew others to her. Saphira was beautiful, and because of her beauty many young warriors frequented the door of his dwelling. Zeram knew he could not keep the warriors at abeyance much longer, for she was more than old enough to wed. Yet he could not bear the thought of her going to any man she did not care for. Because of this Zeram broke tradition and sought her counsel as to who she wished to marry. Yet to the growing consternation of the warriors, and even himself, Saphira was slow to make up her mind.

During their early years Zeram had let Saphira follow him through forests and across streams, showing her where the guinea hens hid their eggs or how to find the best wild berries. She had always been impressed that he knew so much, and though they were the same age—twins by birth—he had become her protector. With the death of their parents a few years ago that role had continued on, and so it seemed that he had been gone too long away from home.

Zeram glancing down at the pottery he held. The craftsmanship was very fine, but what use did he have for a pot like this? Perhaps Saphira would like it, he reflected, for she so often seemed drawn to lovely things. He remembered the colorful flowers and leaves she would find, and the weavings she sometimes made to decorate their dwelling. Saphira would like the pot, though he would not tell her of the maiden who had painted it. Saphira knew the story of the Lamanite victory over the Nephites, and of the women who had begged for mercy, most especially of the one who had bowed before Zeram. Although the telling of it never came from himself, she had asked him several times about the maid who had been brave enough to kneel before him and save her people.

Saphira seemed intrigued by the story, wondering aloud about the girl. Zeram had remained silent on the subject, and his silence had done more to feed her curiosity than if he'd openly told the tale. Although she was shy and usually quiet among the village warriors, Saphira had no shyness while alone with Zeram. She did not hesitate to ask him about the battle.

"She must be very beautiful, this Nephite girl," Saphira had stated one day as she casually handed him his bowl of meat. "I have heard it said that Nephites are a frightening tribe, and that they use trickery and cunning."

"They are weak," Zeram had frowned.

"And ugly, pale like the clouds around a dying moon?" she had asked, repeating a tale often heard.

"Yes."

"Except for this maiden? Ah, I see! You do not answer, my brother. That tells me she was very fair, indeed. Tholar says she had hair like gold. Can such a thing be?"

"Tholar talks too freely."

"You are still mad at Tholar because Jahira wed him," Saphira had teased.

"You know I cared nothing for her."

"She thought fondly of you, as have many maidens. But they grow tired of waiting for you to come from your battles. Yet that is the sorrow of every maiden who feels love for a warrior who only loves war. At least," she said, growing thoughtful, "I have thought so until now. Yet perhaps it is not the battle you love so much, as the memory of this maiden you found in the heart of the battle."

"Have you nothing better to do than pester a man while he tries to eat?" Zeram had growled. "Be gone!"

Saphira had smiled and turned to gather up the cooking pot and utensils. She had said no more on the subject yet his sister knew him too well, Zeram reflected. Often the image of the girl who changed her name to Mara had come to his mind. It was an image he could not erase, and today he had seen her again, though this time it was not in his imagination.

One of the soldiers stopped and ordered two young street urchins to return the warriors' gathered wares to the Lamanite quarters. Zeram handed one of the boys his pot, watching the children scurry away with eyes enlarged by fear.

"Do you have thoughts on what was said by their king?" one of his companions asked as they proceeded down the causeway.

Zeram's mind returned to his meeting with King Limhi. "I am not pleased with the answers given. The Nephite ruler seems to be a just man, yet can any of his kind be trusted to speak the truth?"

The others agreed, and his friend Tholar asked, "What of the testimony of the men who have returned from the wilderness? Do you think they speak the truth?"

"They swear King Noah is dead, burned to death at their own hands.* Their story was clever, but during the battle these men ran as cowards," Zeram answered. "Because of this I am not sure if I can believe their words. Also, King Limhi is Noah's son, and would not wish to see his father dead, even though he has agreed to surrender him to us."

"Perhaps he has instructed his men to depart from the truth in order to save his father's life," another named Corom added.

"Can the words of any man who has acted in such cowardice be believed?" Zeram stated. "What honor did they have, deserting their wives and children to die at the hands of their foe?" He thought of that day again, remembering the maidens who had wept for the lives of their people. Most especially he remembered the one with brown-gold hair who had looked up at him with such trembling courage. Saphira had been right about the appearance of the girl, and he despised any Nephite man who could desert such a maiden.

"I believe our king will accept the Nephite testimony and Limhi's oath of tribute," Tholar said.

"At least in this one thing our captives had been true," Corom stated. "They have delivered up half of all their possessions the first year, and half their gain the year after. A painful price to pay for their weakness."

They nodded in agreement as the men reached a dining chamber where food was being served to other Lamanite soldiers. Zeram would not be joining them since he was to feast with one of the Nephite stewards. He took leave of his

* Mosiah 19:20, 23

companions, heading in the direction of the tribute chambers. His thoughts were still occupied with the events of the day when he turned down the causeway that led to the tribute master's quarters. He felt sudden surprise at seeing the maiden for the second time, and halted.

She appeared deep in thought, her eyes staring at the water channel passing into the city. He felt intrigued that her thoughts so held her that she stood unaware of her surroundings. The late evening light spread amber across the huge stones of the wall and caught threads of color in the maiden's hair. It cast a shadow from her lashes onto her cheek and played darker hues along the gentle curve of her mouth.

Strange that he should see her twice now, when many seasons had passed and he never had before. But, then, the word of his king had not brought him to this city since the day of his victory. He recalled the way she had sat today with the potter's wares, plying her skill. At first when he had passed the place he thought she must be another, a Nephite maiden like all the rest. But then the memory of that long-ago day returned, and he knew the line of brow and cheek that had once been turned up to him in pleading.

He had paused upon seeing her, intent on studying her face. It hadn't been his plan to go to the potter's stall, nor to buy the clay pot, and yet it had happened. He had watched her fingers delicately hold the stylus and move lines of paint on pottery. Even in the act of work her hands had showed a kind of grace that was intriguing. Somehow it had seemed the right thing to do, as if buying the piece of pottery was a kind of truce. Yet the girl had not seemed relieved by his actions. In truth her response had been exactly opposite, though why would it be any other way? To her he must still seem a dangerous foe.

Zeram felt uncertain at seeing her. The maiden was still

graced with beauty, her fairness not diminished by time. If anything she had taken on a more womanly appearance, and yet somehow she appeared different. Now, as then, he had seen fear. Yet on that day the fear had been borne of a deed of courage. This fear seemed a haunted one.

For the first time he felt unsure of his victory over his foe. Then he reminded himself that his king had been generous with the people of Limhi, for some warriors still murmured against the decision. He moved closer, studying her.

Mara's thoughts were disrupted by the sound of footsteps and she turned, glancing up at the man who approached. She didn't try to hide what she felt, taking a slight step back. The chance meeting this afternoon suddenly turned this moment into one of threat. She studied him warily. Despite the pounding of her heart Mara forced herself to stand her ground although every instinct told her to flee. This time she didn't lower her eyes in submission. Instead the anger within her allowed her to openly face him. He stood before her, looking down with his near-black eyes. And yet his height was not ominous, the way she remembered at their first meeting on that first day when she had knelt before him and he had seemed to tower above her. Mara couldn't read his expression, thinking that his stern countenance showed only disapproval.

"Why do you come here?" she asked.

The straightforwardness of her question surprised him. "I am here at the request of my king."

His words had little meaning for her, but his voice caught her attention. Although their peoples shared the same tongue, each had different inflections because of the many years the two groups had lived apart. Yet she had heard the words of other Lamanites, and none held the somber tones of quiet strength that his did.

She composed herself, aware that his eyes never left her. "What has that to do with me?"

He said nothing, his look a question.

"For what reason do you approach me?" she asked.

"Chance brought me to the marketplace today. And here."

Mara paused, wondering if he did not remember her from that day so long ago. If that were so, then she had erred in speaking so quickly. She made the sign of apology and turned to leave.

"Mara."

The sound of him calling her by name made her turn back, her eyes wide. "How can you speak my name?" she asked in a low voice.

Zeram understood her question. She didn't understand how he knew her name. A slight smile touched his lips. "Do you forget my presence there, at the place of your mourning?"

Mara took in a sharp breath, realizing that he did remember, that he even remembered things she had almost forgotten. She thought of the night when she mourned the death of her fathers and the captivity of her people. He had been there when she changed her name, a sign of her bitter sorrow. Strange emotions welled up inside her. This Lamanite warrior had been part of her suffering, part of her saving. He had spared her life and yet had seen her mourning.

He looked down at her with eyes she couldn't read. "You need not be afraid," he stated in such a low voice she felt uncertain she had heard him. "Why do you fear the one who once saved your life?"

"Saved my life?" she whispered harshly, as if he had done no act of kindness at all.

"Your life, and those of the people your king and his men abandoned," he reminded.

Something in these last words hurt her, he could see it

in the line of her mouth. Then he remembered her cry from long ago, the few words spoken that had told him how her own father had left her to die. He didn't like the way this made him feel, the softening which made him grow weak. He hid his feelings, turning away from her. "Leave this place," he commanded.

His gaze followed her as she hurried away, fleeing from him as if running for her very life. In a moment she had disappeared from view. Zeram stalked away, leaving the courtyard and heading toward the tribute chambers.

CHAPTER THREE

F ar from the city of Nephi, beyond the pool of volcanic glass and hillsides thick with white-bark trees, a group of renegade Nephites lay in hiding. Samuel peered over the edge of the high ground where he and the others hid. The hillside sloped down into a green vale beside the river, a small meadow sheltered by a knoll on one side and trees on the other. Sunlight filtered through the branches of the trees along the bank, shimmering on the leaves and rushing water.

The young man paid little heed to the serene setting below, instead his eyes followed the movements of the maidens. He watched their dancing with fascination, and listened to the sound of their singing which drifted back across the hill. It had been a long time since he and the others had seen such play, yet even though intrigued by what he saw, the same sense of helpless dread he had felt so often in the past returned.

"Let us go now!" one of them said eagerly.

Samuel turned his head to look down the line of men and recognized Jubal, a Zoramite by descent, and one of the priests he had always despised. The hard rigors of living in the wilderness had hardly diminished the man's girth. He only appeared more cruel, his small eyes ever watching.

"Not yet," the low voice of their leader said. "Wait until more have left. There are too many, still."

Samuel glanced over at the priest who had taken control of their band. Amulon* had sharp features and quick,

* Mosiah 23:31-32

cunning eyes that trusted no one. A man full of power, he had done little to intervene with the death of their king, instead taking up the new role of leader with ease. Of all the priests, Samuel disliked him the most. He looked back at the maidens who made merry, his own heart sinking.

Heshlon nudged his son. "There, Samuel. Look at the maiden with the timbrel. That one should be for you, eh?"

He ignored his father's gesture. "If we do this, will the Lamanites war against the remnant of our people?" he asked.

Others glanced over at him, disdain in their hardened expressions. Heshlon scowled. "What shall we do? We live in the wilderness and can never return to our homes."

"The others went back," Samuel stated in a quiet voice.

Amulon turned to him with a smile of patient annoyance. "Is that what you believe? It is my guess they never reached the city of Nephi, or if they did their blood was spilled by our foe. Certainly the Lamanites destroyed every one of our kinsmen."

Samuel had heard the same argument before and sighed in frustration. "You do not know that. Perhaps our brethren triumphed over the enemy. They have done so in the past. I do not believe it is our fear which keeps us from returning home, but instead our shame."

Amulon's smile faded and he scowled at the son of his friend. Resentment etched the faces of the other priests but Samuel didn't look away. "We bear the shame of deserting our people, and now you wish to add to it by stealing the daughters of the Lamanites."

"The Lamanites are our foe!" Jubal hissed.

"Does that make our actions right? This is not war."

"What has right to do with it?" the other asked, staring at him in irritation.

Samuel ignored his father's hand on his arm. Instead he

laughed, a low, bitter sound. "You are priests! When you reigned under King Noah was your calling to that position only pretense?"

Cumeni, one who had remained silent until now, sneered at Heshlon. "Does your child seek to counsel us?"

Heshlon looked away in shame and Samuel knew he had dishonored his father. Amulon stared at the young man long and hard. "You could have fled with the others when they slayed the king. Why did you stay?"

"I wish I had not," Samuel replied.

"Then leave! Return to the ruins of the city if that is your wish."

Jubal gave a furtive nod. "I agree! Let him go back."

"No!" Heshlon said, his startled voice too loud.

Amulon signaled him to be silent, continuing on in his own low voice. "If you did go back, Samuel, you would die, and that is not my wish. You have become like a son to me, since surely my own sons are now dead. Yet if we take these maidens we may have families of our own so that our race will not be destroyed."

"An honorable task," Samuel answered bitterly.

Amulon's eyes narrowed but he chuckled. Reaching out he clasped the young man on the neck with a firm grasp. "Pick out which of the maidens you would have, and when their numbers have diminished we shall go down the hill."

Samuel pulled away, lying on his stomach and peering over the edge of the hill. His father moved beside him. "Son," he whispered, his voice saddened. "Why do you shame me in front of the others?"

He wanted to respond that they shamed themselves, but out of honor to his father he would not say it. Heshlon sighed. "Were you earnest in your words? That you wish you had not stayed with me when the others departed?"

Samuel didn't look at his father, hating to speak that which would cause hurt, yet unable to do anything else. "Yes. And more than that. I would that I had stayed with my people, even if I should have died with them."

The words, spoken at last, drained him and he had no desire left to look at his father. Instead he thought back to the day of the war. He could still feel the fear, could see the terror in King Noah's eyes. Why had his father and the others listened to a man of such cowardice? Couldn't they see what he was? Samuel remembered his own decision in fleeing the battle: First, the short span of indecision from the other men before they fled; hesitation, watching his people and the enemy below; his father following the king, urging Samuel to come; the uncertainty about what to do. His mother and sister had died of the fever, and all he had left was his father. Two years ago he had followed. Then he had been a boy, now he had become a man. The only consolation he received came from knowing that if he had to make the decision again today he would choose differently, while Amulon and the rest would act just the same.

The time that followed their flight had become exceedingly difficult. Over the ensuing seasons regret plagued him, and plagued the other laymen as well. When they had finally decided to return to the land of Nephi, regardless of what fate they would meet, he had been glad of it. He remembered the demands of King Noah, his ranting orders that angered the Nephite men. They had killed him and then had sought the lives of the priests.* Once again Samuel had fled, not fearing for his own life but that of his father. Twice he had made the wrong choice, and now faced with a third the bitterness of the moment choked him.

He wondered what had happened to these men who once wore the blue robes and jeweled ephods of their important

* Mosiah 19:19-21

role. Had they always been a shallow counterfeit pretending to the priesthood? The people of Noah once looked up to them as leaders, yet these same men had abandoned those people. And most had even deserted wives and children. He glanced over at Cumeni, once one of the most powerful priests in the king's court. He had left behind a daughter. Samuel couldn't recall her name, but remembered she had been most fair. Had it hurt Cumeni to do such a deed? Samuel could not tell. Sadly he wondered if Amulon's words were true, that all the people of Nephi were destroyed.

"See," Heshlon said at last, his light tone belying the hurt he still felt. "There is one who is exceeding fair. I spied her before. She would make you a fine wife."

Samuel studied the maiden his father pointed out, his worries fading for the moment. Heshlon was right in one thing, her fairness rivaled any.

The maiden carried a timbrel, tapping it lightly and moving in rhythm. She bore such a natural grace that Samuel could do nothing but stare at her, studying the fluid line of face and form. Clothed in a tunic of scarlet, her hands following the arc of the dance, she seemed the very center of the play. Her long black hair was caught up in a silver circlet and a few straight wisps fell across her brow and cheek. Laughter didn't come so easily to her lips, the merriment of the others only making her smile.

When the dance ended, several of the maidens lifted their hands in farewell, departing from the circle. She didn't leave, however. Samuel watched her stand beside some of the others, speaking words he couldn't hear. Since he had not seen a woman for many seasons, he felt intrigued by watching her. When she spoke she used her hands with the same delicate grace as when she danced.

Samuel, caught up in his study of her, didn't see the signal given. He was not aware of the intentions of the men until he saw them leap over the top of the hill.*

Saphira smiled at the playful words of the other maidens but didn't answer, instead she looked down at the timbrel in her hands. They teased her about a warrior who spoke of marriage to her kinsman, and she felt the difficulty of the moment. They took her words of protest to mean acceptance and she felt frustrated in her denial of their assumptions. When the others were finally ready to depart she felt relieved that they no longer put their attentions on her.

She and the others had turned in the direction of their homeland when a piercing scream startled them, the laughter dying. One of the maidens pointed in horror towards the top of the hill.

Saphira stared at the sight, uncertainty making her unable to move. Strange men ran down the hill towards them, and though they wielded no weapons still she felt threatened. She caught a glimpse of fierce expressions, of animal skins covering tattered tunics, and knew these men were not of her people. She turned, fleeing with the others, and the timbrel fell from her hand. The fear of being chased filled her with panic and she ran blindly, only knowing they were trapped between the river and their pursuers.

Samuel watched, stunned, as the men bolted down the hill, descending on the maidens like hawks attacking prey. He listened to the screams of terror and suddenly leapt over the edge shouting angry, unheard protests. He ran down the

* Mosiah 20:1-5

incline to find himself amid the turmoil, shouting at them to stop, his hands clenched into angry fists. The helplessness of the moment engulfed him, since they were many and he was only one.

A piercing scream caught his attention and he looked to the river. He saw a movement of scarlet and recognized the tunic of the maiden he had been watching. Jubal had followed her to the river, and with surprising speed for one of his girth, the priest grabbed her hair with one quick movement and jerked her back to the shore. Samuel felt his face go hot from rage and he bolted forward.

Saphira half crawled up the shore, her feet slipping on the clay bank as the man dragged her out of the river. Once out of the water she gasped for air, forced to kneel at his feet. His hand cruelly pulled her head back, the pain of his grasp on her hair causing a sob to escape her. She stared up into small, cruel eyes in the man's round face, his knowing grin making her heart sink. His face had no shred of mercy or kindness, and a terrible dread filled her, making her tremble.

A loud war cry split the air, and Saphira's head jerked back even further by the man's grasp being knocked away. Suddenly, free of his hold, she stared in awe at the scene before her. Another man of slighter build had thrown himself full force against her enemy who sprawled on the ground. Nearly half her attacker's weight, the slighter man had prevailed by the blind surprise of the moment and the intense force with which he had thrown himself into the act. In a moment he had sprung up again, avoiding the fat one who faced him with murderous hatred in his eyes.

Saphira leapt to her feet but another man grabbed her wrist, holding her prisoner with a second maiden. A large man with an iron grip, he held her so tightly that she couldn't escape no matter how she fought.

Samuel faced Jubal, his opponent livid with rage. It was this very rage which made his movements predictable and enabled the younger man to outmaneuver him. Jubal lunged at Samuel who moved quickly aside, sending a heavy blow across his shoulders. Jubal lost his balance, falling to the earth. Yet when he arose a knife of black obsidian glinted wickedly in his grasp. The heavier man crouched, ready for attack, a vicious snarl on his lips. For the first time fear touched Samuel. He faced his foe, anticipating the quick thrusts of the knife with surprising skill.

Samuel, intense on avoiding the deathly sharp implement, didn't see Amulon thrust the maiden he held to another. Neither opponent saw the leader approach until Jubal felt the knife kicked from his hand. He howled in pain, his face discolored with rage.

Amulon sent a quick glance at the younger man who straightened, facing the two priests. Jubal, finding his voice, choked out oaths of rage. "Let me kill him!"

The leader stayed him. "Even unarmed, Samuel has triumphed over you. Let him have the maiden."

"No!"

Amulon faced the other priest, towering over him. "It is my decision," he said in a low voice that held a deadly threat.

Jubal knew Amulon well enough to fear him and he felt his stand weakening. He tried to protest, but his wrist still ached from the blow it had received. "The maiden should be mine, it is I who had hold of her first! Ask the others. Will you not agree with me?" he cried, pleading his cause to the other men who looked away. None of them cared to argue with their leader's authority, for, except for their king, they had not known such a fiercely cruel man.

"You had hold of her first," Amulon stated. "But it is Samuel who took her from you. He has triumphed."

"You would give that boy reign over me?" Jubal choked.

"He is more of a man than you know," Amulon said.

He walked over to Cumeni who held two struggling maidens, taking hold of the one clothed in scarlet. With one quick movement he thrust her toward Samuel, who looked startled.

Amulon threw back his head in laughter. "So we see our cub has become a lion." All of the men, except for two, laughed—Samuel, who, feeling the fearful trembling of the maiden within his grasp, felt fresh anger at the sound of merriment entwined with the bitter weeping of the Lamanite daughters, and Jubal, who stared at the younger man, his eyes narrowing in hatred. The Zoramite walked to where his knife lay and stooped to pick it up.

"Let us move with haste," Amulon commanded. "If their fathers find us our lives will be forfeit."

At his order the priests began to ascend the hill, dragging their prey into the wilderness.

Saphira continued to fight against her captor despite the exhaustion that nearly overtook her. The farther they traveled from the river, the more desperate she felt the need to escape. The other maidens also fought, and some were struck by the men who dragged them along.

Amulon raised his hand, signaling the others to halt. Looking back in the direction they had come he could still see the top of the hill in the distance. Their progress was slow, for the women fought with surprising determination. Occasionally one would break free, and one of the men would have to pursue her, which slowed the progress of the group considerably.

Amulon untied some strips of leather which hung from

his belt and tossed one to each man. "Bind them," he commanded. "If we do not hasten out of the land of Shemlon, the Lamanites will be upon us."

The men quickly caught up the thongs and began the work despite the struggling protests of their captives. Samuel paused for a moment, not wanting to bind the maiden's wrists and yet knowing he couldn't keep up with the others if he didn't. Despite her delicate frame, she displayed surprising strength and determination. With every step she had fought him, striking him if he didn't hold her hands.

When Saphira saw his intent to bind her, panic filled her and she jerked her hand away with the strength she had left, breaking free. She leapt away and in a moment he was after her. She ran with all the swift speed of a terrified doe, and yet he followed so closely she could hear his breathing.

Samuel pushed himself with all the strength he could summon, knowing if he fell behind she would be gone. The maiden ran swiftly, until he leapt through the air, grabbing her. They tumbled to the ground, gasping for breath, and before she could twist free of him he caught her wrists, wrapping the leather band about them.

Terror blinded Saphira at being bound and she bent her head, biting his hand. She expected the blow to come that would knock her away. When it didn't she pulled back, looking up at her captor. His face was grim and glancing down at his hand where her teeth had sunk into the fleshy part of his hand beneath the thumb, she saw she had drawn blood.

After he had finished knotting the leather, he stood, lifting her to her feet to return to the others. Ahead of them the men dragged her sisters along, some of them pulling on the long cord left from the knots. One of the maidens fell and her captor so cruelly jerked her to her feet that she cried out.

"We must keep up with them," Samuel said.

Saphira started at the sound of his voice. His face still grim, he didn't look down at her when he spoke. "If you do not try to flee, I will let go of the cord."

When he glanced down at her she looked away. Samuel released the tie, which allowed her hands to rest from being outstretched. Saphira thought that perhaps she could flee, but knew that if he had managed to catch her when her hands were untied, there would be no chance with them bound. Instead she hastened to match his stride, not wanting to be dragged along in the manner many of the others were.

Saphira looked up at her captor whose countenance was unlike any she had known. For the first time she saw how he differed even from his own men. His age was near her own, while many of the men were a number of years older. And although not of a heavy build, still he bore the strength of one who lived and survived in the wilds.

She had never seen anyone like him, for his appearance was not like the men in her land. His hair didn't have the dark cast to it of her own people. Instead it was fair, the light plying its brown hue with golden threads, while his skin bore a lighter hue than the bronze color of the men in her land. Suddenly her eyes widened in amazement. These strangers were the hated foe of her people. Nephites!

The word hissed like a curse in her mind, making her heart recoil in fear. She had heard of his kind, had been told tales about the dreaded foe, but until this day had never seen one. She now understood why her people spoke of them with hatred, for hadn't their actions proven the truth this very day? Her mouth tasted bitter at the thought that her brother had once spared these people who now doled out such treachery.

Samuel felt the maiden's eyes upon him and he looked down at her. The expression she wore before she looked away was one of contempt, and he felt his heart sink. "She has every right to despise me," he thought unhappily. He looked at the scarlet tunic she wore, its damp hem soiled and torn. Her black hair fell unbound, the silver circlet lost along the way. Her face bore smudges of dirt, and yet despite everything she appeared more beautiful to him than when he had watched her from afar.

He continued to study her, knowing she must be growing weary and yet she still forced herself to keep the pace. Something in her expression made him believe she had resigned herself for the moment, but he had no doubt she would try to escape again.

After a space of time they came across a shallow rill, stopping to drink and rest. Samuel felt weary from all he had been through and he wondered about the maidens and how they could travel so far over such difficult land. Many seemed near collapsing when they were finally able to ease their thirst and rest by the small river. After only a short rest, however, Amulon ordered them to continue on, ever mindful of the fierce Lamanites who would certainly seek their lost daughters.

How long they walked Saphira couldn't tell, knowing only that the day grew old. In the distance low hills bore shadows in deep crevices, presenting a timeworn, wrinkled face upon the land. The sun sank low behind the bluffs, streaking the sky with crimson. Still the small band continued to trudge towards the hills that loomed before them.

Apprehension filled Saphira and with all her being she hoped that the warriors of her people would be able to follow. Her mind turned to her brother. "Oh, if Zeram were only here!" she sighed inwardly. Certainly he would save her from these despised Nephite men.

By the time the priests reached the face of the bluff, darkness had spread its shadowed wings across the mountain. Amulon led his men into a shallow cavity where they sank down on rough pelts. The women huddled together, low, fearful whispers passing among them.

Hathomi, a maiden several seasons older than Saphira, clutched at her arm. "Saphira. . . ."

The younger girl turned to her friend. "These men are Nephites," she whispered.

"Yes, it is so," Hathomi answered in a low voice. "Have our fathers not taught of the deceit of our foe? They do not act as warriors, but as thieves who would steal us from our land."

"Will our kinsmen save us?" she whispered.

"Perhaps, if we travel no further. But the one who is their leader is not foolish. I fear he will take us far away until we cannot return to our homeland," Hathomi answered miserably.

Saphira wanted to say more, but fearing her captors she only peered around the shallow indent in the hill. She didn't believe this was the dwelling place of these men, but that they had only hidden their food and skins here.

The priests slaked their thirsts from water skins while she and the other maidens watched. Saphira glanced over at the young man who held her captive, watching him drink. He lowered the water skin, cast his glance in her direction, then handed the heavy water bag to her. Despite the difficulty of lifting the bag with her hands tied, she managed. Though warm, the water still relieved her parched throat. Quickly she passed it to Hathomi and the other maidens.

At the mouth of the hole, a cooking fire had burned down to coals and one of the men pulled back charred leaves. Inside meat dripped with juice, hissing on the coals, and the men eagerly eased their hunger. When they were sated they offered the maidens food, growing jovial in discussing their

exploits. Many of them grew boastful about the success of
the venture, yet Samuel thought that triumphing over a group
of unarmed women displayed only foolishness.

He handed some meat to Saphira who struggled to force
down a few mouthfuls. She ate in silence, her eyes continuing to study her surroundings. Finally she leaned near the
youngest maiden.

"Ura, you must eat."

"I cannot," Ura whispered, choking back a sob.

"You must. How will you have the strength to escape?"
she murmured in a voice barely audible to the other maiden.

Ura's eyes widened slightly. "How," she mouthed.

"You must watch and wait. Perhaps tomorrow they
will grow careless."

A sudden form loomed above them, the slight glow from
the embers outlining his frame. Saphira realized it was the
leader. She saw him motion to the young man who kept watch
over her and heard him say, "Samuel, you had best watch
your woman. She may be plotting to escape." He reached
down, catching hold of Saphira's arm, and shoved her towards Samuel. A gasp escaped her at his roughness, and she
moved instinctively beside the younger man, who had shown
some kindness to her. Behind her, Ura scurried towards the
wall where the man who had captured her sat, fearing him
less than the Nephite leader.

"Keep hold on your women," the leader ordered his men.
"I would bind them to you before you rest. At first light we
depart."

Saphira shuddered, fear and anger possessing her.
However, once the anger faded, hopelessness replaced it.
Tomorrow they would again resume the journey, traveling farther into the wilderness. What hope was there that
their kinsmen might arrive to fight for them? She leaned

her back against the cold stone of the cave, her heart heavy with misery.

Samuel studied her in the deepening light. He wanted to tell her that he had protested against stealing her and her sisters away, yet knew his very actions condemned him. He thought about what had happened, wondering at the blind rage which had caused him to attack Jubal and fight for her. He hadn't planned to steal her from her people, but seeing the Zoramite's cruel abuse of her had caused him to react in a manner unlike anything he had done before.

Saphira returned the gaze of the one called Samuel. She stared at him with all the disdain she felt for his kind. Finally he looked away, not wanting to see the open hostility she displayed. She felt somewhat bewildered by this action and looked around at the other Nephite men. Across from her sat the other man, the one which the Nephite Samuel had fought. She remembered the vicious way the fat one had grabbed her hair, dragging her from the river and forcing her to her knees. His shadowed face appeared doubly cruel, his small eyes piercing her. He didn't see her looking at him, and she watched as his eyes flicked with quick, snakelike movements toward the young man beside her. Hatred made his features sharp and at the expression on his face, a feeling of cold dread filled her.

For the moment she was guarded by the younger of the two. If the one named Samuel had not fought for her, would she now be in the grasp of the cruel one? The thought nearly made her ill. Would this other one have borne the pain of her bite and done nothing? His gaze shifted to her and feeling his eyes upon her, she could sense the wickedness in him. It was quite evident that he hated the younger man. Were he to kill Samuel, would she then be handed over to him again?

Samuel, too, had been studying Jubal. The priest had

always treated him with contempt, which had now grown into hatred. In fighting for the Lamanite maiden Samuel had made a foe, one who could be dangerous. He had also gone against the very things he believed to be right and in doing so helped change the lives of those who were innocent.

He felt the maiden's eyes on him again and pulled himself from his thoughts, looking down at her. In the near darkness he seemed to detect an expression of alarm. He even thought she wished to speak to him, but the moment passed and she lowered her head. He motioned to the stiff pelt he had slept on the previous night.

"Lie down and sleep if you can. Tomorrow we travel into a desolate place."

His words echoed through Saphira's very being. Her heart empty, she lay down on the pelt. She could hear the muffled weeping of the other maidens and her heart made the same sound, though her lips were still. At last Samuel stretched himself out beside her. Aware of his near presence, even though he didn't touch her, Saphira stared into the blackness.

She knew he had tied the long end of her binding to the sash of his tunic. Patiently she waited for the rhythmic sound of his breathing, then slowly she began to twist the leather band that bound her wrists, struggling to work her hands free. Her only hope lay in the chance that she might escape her bond and captors before first light.

CHAPTER FOUR

With the coming of dawn, Lamanite warriors returned to the lea at the edge of the land of Shemlon. The eve before they had carried torches into the place but darkness had greatly hampered their search, forcing them to wait in helplessness until first light. Silence filled the air with foreboding while Zeram and the others studied the ground. In the damp earth there were still a few impressions left by the feet of the attackers, smooth marks made by shod feet. Zeram looked across the hill, seeing the dense foliage beyond. Whoever had stolen the maidens had taken them into the wilderness, and trying to follow would be an almost impossible task.

Grimly Zeram walked to the river bank where something caught his eye. He stooped, picking up a timbrel. The decorative threads were caked with mud, some of the shells broken, yet still he recognized it, having seen it used in dance. He felt a cold knot in the very core of his being, a terrible dread that welled up inside him. He didn't want to believe this was Saphira's timbrel, did not want to recognize it, even as the truth became evident.

His whole life he had been a warrior, a man without fear. Yet now he was afraid. He thought of Saphira, so much smaller than himself, so gentle even when she was playful. Always until now he had kept her safe, protected her from everything. He was a soldier of action, yet now he felt helpless. Who had done this thing!

Rage coursed through Zeram and his hands clenched

into fists. The muscles of his chest became taut and he threw his head back and let forth a scream of rage that echoed across the vale.

The eyes of the others were on him, and when his terrible war cry had ended he reached down to the dark mud along the river's course. Dipping his fingers into the clay he stood, making the mark of war upon his forehead. Then he faced the others, his rage infecting them. King Laman stared at Zeram, then he also placed the black mark on his brow, and the others followed.

The Lamanite king raised his voice in command. "Let us gather at the place of weapons where we will make cimeters and arrows. Then we will march on the city of Nephi and destroy it!"

A shout went up from the warriors and Zeram raised his fist with the others. He wanted revenge. He wanted to destroy the Nephites who had done this. Most of all, though, he wanted Saphira back, unharmed and safe. If it meant destroying every Nephite, and leaving no single stone of the city wall standing, he would do it!*

Mara roused before first light. Outside the window the position of the moon told her that dawn would soon edge the horizon. She felt immediately alert, knowing the time had come. She stood and quickly donned her warmest tunic. The night's sleep had been slow in coming, and fitful, because of her plans. Part of her had wanted to flee with the coming of night, yet she forced herself to be patient. Once outside the city walls it would have been far too dark to travel across the land.

Uncertainty made her feel empty, a hollow echoing

* Mosiah 20:6

through her body caused by excitement and fear. Hurriedly she spread her shawl on the ground, folding her other tunic and placing it on the square of cloth. Then she wrapped up the goat cheese and parched corn she had traded for at the market. Tying the ends of the fabric together she stood, glancing about the small circular chamber. For a moment Mara hesitated. Despite the unhappiness she had known since the captivity of her people, she wondered if the course now chosen would bring her even further sorrow.

Mara cast the thought aside. Even old Benjamin had told her often that one day there would be no place left for her at the potter's stand. When she didn't come to do her tasks this morning Mahijah would be angry. She hoped that his anger would keep him from sending Oriah to look for her, at least until tomorrow. Yet should he come today it wouldn't matter. Who would believe that a mere woman such as herself would try to escape the city? They wouldn't know for several days, and by then she hopefully would have reached the people of Alma.

Catching up her head cloth, Mara tied it across her brow, tucking her hair beneath the fold. Then she went to a place in the wall, feeling for the familiar oval stone. After a few moments of working it back and forth the stone loosened and came away into her hands. She felt inside the black recess for the precious item until her fingers found it and caught it up.

Unable to see it in the dim light, still her fingers caressed the small surface of finely carved gold. Her mind saw what her fingers felt, a simple piece of hammered gold carved in the shape of a single glyph and hung on a silk cord. Her only precious possession now, Riplah had given it to her during one of his lessons.

"Oh, how lovely!" she had cried.

"Keep it always safe, my child, for it holds a greater sig-nificance than you can know." Riplah had put it into her hand and wrapping her fingers around it, his thin and knobby fingers encircling her own. Mara paused only a moment in the memory of it.

Although all her other jewels and fine raiment had been traded for food and coin, Mara had refused to part with this small treasure of her heart. Although she had gleaned the fields in her attempts to assuage the pain of hunger, still she hadn't sold it.

Quickly she slipped the cord over her head, letting the glyph slip inside her tunic where it felt cold against her skin. Then she gathered up the small bundle and slipped out into the open causeway. Once outside the cool air touched her face and she peered at the dim outline of the city, gray against a black sky. Feeling her way along the high stone wall she moved down the path her mind had taken many times dur-ing the night. After reaching the open court she took in a slow breath, her heart pounding. Part of her desperately wanted to return to the safety and warmth of her small cham-ber, to climb on the pallet and sleep until dawn. Yet Mara reminded herself that since her decision to flee the city, no bad dreams had haunted her, nor had she felt the hopeless weight that had lain for so long upon her breast.

Determined, she hurried to the place where the viaduct merged with the stone wall. Pausing for only a moment she slipped the tied ends of the shawl over her neck so that her hands would be free of the bundle. Not allowing further thought Mara stepped down into the water, sucking in her breath. The cold water swirled past her, the channel deep, rising nearly to her shoulders.

It was difficult for Mara to work her way along the via-duct against the swift flow of the stream. She touched the outer city wall, her hands feeling for the curved top of the viaduct which the water surged beneath. Fear nearly overcame her, the black rush of water beneath the thick stones ominously frightening. Not pausing to think, knowing that if she did following her course would become too great a task, she took in a deep breath and sank down into the water.

The cold depths surrounded her face, her hands feeling along the curved stones overhead. She struggled against the force of the water where it rushed through the narrow spillway, threatening to push her back through.

Carefully she felt her way with her feet and hands, yet half way through the bundle tied around her neck caught on something and held her. Panic filled Mara as she pulled with all her might to be free. Air escaped her lips and water surged into her mouth. In one desperate try she lunged forward, her bundle pulling free. She surfaced, her head hitting the outside edge of the wall. In a moment she began choking in air and coughing out water. Her numb fingers clung to the edge of the viaduct even as the force of the water threatened to push her back through the opening. Using the last strength in her arms Mara pulled herself from the water, the weight of the soaked garments nearly dragging her down.

She lay on the edge of the stone bank, gasping in air, the city's outer wall looming beside her. Her stiff fingers rubbed the blur of water from her eyes. Overhead the ebony sky paled to gray on the horizon, the moon a faint shadow on the opposite edge of the expanse. After the weakness had passed Mara dragged herself to her feet, shivering in the cold air that chilled her wet clothing. Her eyes scanned the top of the wall and her heart eased slightly because she could see no watchman was ready to cry out.

Turning away from the city she moved across the fields of tall grain, fearful someone might see her. Mara knew that this was the greatest danger, since the fields were wide and gave no shelter. She tried to crouch low to be hidden by the tall grain, and in the growing light she could see the edge of forest. It became her aim. If only she could reach the trees without being seen!

She ran for a long while, then paused to catch her breath and bind up the soaked hem of her tunic to allow her easier movement. Her eyes scanned the dim horizon, studying each point where she expected Lamanites to stand guard.* She saw no warriors and new fears stung her. Where were the guards who watched the borders of Nephi? Perhaps she had misjudged their watchpoints when she studied them from the city wall. Despite her travel southward from the city there was no sign of the guards. Had she erred in the placement of them now that she stood outside the city? Another thought jolted her. What if the Lamanite soldiers had seen her escape and even now closed in?

Mara cast aside all caution, turning and fleeing towards the forest in a straight line. The cold no longer plagued her and she didn't think again about returning to the city. Instead she fled, her eyes on the line of forest, and in a moment found herself among the shelter of branches. She paused, listening to detect if anyone followed, yet nothing reached her ears but the sound of a slight wind in the trees and the rustle of forest animals.

Despite the growing light it was dark in the forest and Mara moved cautiously. She walked over fallen trees and among thick brush, branches scratching her face and arms and pulling at her tunic. Deep in the forest she looked back, seeing no sign of the fields she had left. Her arms and legs felt weak and she sank down, pulling the soaked bundle from around her neck. She set it aside and then lay down on a moss patch beneath a fallen tree, the muscles in her arms and legs aching.

* Mosiah 19:27-29

Exhaustion filled Mara, but still her heart felt light. She had triumphed! She had escaped and fulfilled, in part, the oath made long ago to her beloved Riplah. Something inside her eased for the first time in many seasons. If she could rest for a short while she would then travel through the forest and seek the place of refuge.

A faint gray glow in the distance heralded morning when Heshlon roused his son. Samuel sat up, hardly awake. "You sleep too soundly," his father chuckled.

Samuel said nothing, glancing down at the maiden beside him. His father nodded. "She will be good for you, my son."

Samuel shook his head in discouragement.

"She despises me," he replied in a low voice.

Heshlon smiled slightly. "They all do. Yet in time, when they have forgotten the land of their fathers and have accepted us in the place of their kinsmen, they will hate us no more. Then we will find a place to live, and dwell with them as husband and wife."

Samuel shook his head with sadness. "They will never forget. Have we forgotten those left behind?"

Heshlon didn't know how to answer his son, so when Amulon spoke to his men to rouse, he turned away. Moving across the floor of the cavity, he placed his hand on the maiden called Hathomi to awaken her.

Saphira started at the sound of voices, lifting her eyes to peer up into the face of her captor. "We are departing," he said.

She sat up, pushing back her hair as best she could with her hands bound. He helped her to her feet, stooping to roll up the pelt. Her heart felt heavy and she looked down at her wrists. The hours of struggling to pull free of the leather cord had only rubbed her flesh raw. Her wrists were swollen and she had less chance of escaping than before.

The group left the mountain, moving out into the early morning air. Amulon signaled them in the direction they should take and the men followed him into the wilderness, leading away the captive Lamanite daughters.

They traveled beyond the hills and into the dense brush of wilderness, struggling through the heavy foliage. Moving upwards they journeyed into a forest of trees that filtered slender beams of light through the branches. The cries of startled parrots and wild doves echoed strangely through the forest, the air cool beneath the high branches.

Saphira carefully picked her way along the sponge-like ground, watchful where her bare feet trod. Her mind labored to remember the way so that if she escaped she could find her way back to the land of Shemlon. But with each twist and turn, unable to watch the movement of the sun because of the trees, her hopes began to fail. In the distance there was the sound of rushing water and the forest floor fell away at the edge of a ravine. A small river twisted among the foliage and the group climbed down to its rock-strewn edge. Taking a moment to rest and quench their thirst, they also filled the water skins.

Saphira gazed up at the sky where it broke free of the overhead trees, studying the late morning sun. She wondered what direction they had come, but couldn't discern if they had traveled strictly southward or not. Nor could she guess how far they had come. This was a new river, smaller than the one by which she and the other maidens had come to make merry. All about her the land seemed strange, and she felt lost. Even if she were to escape, could she make her way back to the homeland? Her heart felt heavy at the thought.

She stooped down to try and cup water with her bound hands, yet when the thongs strained at her wrists she winced. Samuel looked up from the stream where he finished filling a water skin, bound the end and stood, slinging the bag to his shoulder. Then he looked at her, studying her face framed by the black hair that had glints of blue beneath the morning sun. His eyes trailed to the binding. He lifted her hands, studying the place where her flesh had grown raw from trying to escape the bonds. A scowl darkened his brow and he looked into her face.

"You tried to get free," he stated.

She said nothing, only returned his gaze as if she hadn't heard him. In a moment Amulon called out to the men to travel on, yet when the others moved away Samuel continued to stand, facing her.

"If I cut the bindings will you swear an oath that you will not flee?"

Saphira turned, watching the others leave. "Would you have me speak an oath I cannot keep?"

Samuel felt surprised at her words. He hadn't heard her speak before and the low sound of her voice and what she said filled him with uncertainty. He hesitated then reached into his belt. Pulling out a small piece of sharp obsidian he sliced through the binding. Then casting it aside he signaled to her to kneel beside the stream. The freedom of having the bindings cut filled her with great relief and she did what he bade. Samuel knelt beside her and dipped down into the river, pouring the cool water over her wrists.

"I do not see the healing plant here," he stated at last, helping her stand. "When I find it we can use the leaves for a salve."

Saphira looked at him, bewildered. "You treat me with kindness, and yet your kinsmen have stolen us from our people."

Samuel struggled to find the right words. "I spoke against carrying you and your sisters away, but the others took my words for naught."

They walked along in silence, Saphira thinking about what he had said. "Why have you cut my bindings without my giving an oath? Do you not know I shall flee?"

"Yes, I know it." He looked down at her. "I did not seek to take you for myself. It was only when I saw Jubal carry you away. . . ." His voice trailed off and he looked aside.

"Is this the way, with the men of Nephi?"

She was surprised by the vehemence of his reply. "No! Amulon and the others are wicked men who fled with their king, deserting their people when your brethren warred with us."

Saphira thought about this, and all the things which he had spoken. He willingly admitted the wrongdoing of his kinsmen and she sensed the shame he felt. "How did you come to be with them?"

Samuel bowed his head. "The one called Heshlon is my father."

She thought he would speak no more, but then he said hesitantly, "You are called Saphira."

She questioned him with her eyes and he smiled. "I heard one of the other maidens speak your name."

Saphira didn't answer him and the silence grew between them. She thought that she had spoken too easily and should guard herself against trusting him. Every step they took led her away from all she loved and knew. And now, with her hands unbound, the Nephite had given her the chance she needed. Perhaps there would be a way if this Samuel grew careless.

In the hushed stirrings of the forest her mind continued to work, knowing that she now might escape. Her scheme, like a smoldering ember, need only wait for the right moment to burst into life.

CHAPTER FIVE

A soft haze of light spread itself across the forest, deepening the shadowed greens of foliage and trees. Sapotes and mahoganies towered above the shorter cedars and palms, the separate hues of their green leaves layered together in an emerald mixture. Mara slowly opened her eyes, staring into the forest thick with vines and moss. In the distance filtered rays of morning light fanned out like fine hammered gold, brightening all the places they lit upon.

Slowly a smile touched her lips, her heart feeling as if it had been set free, a bird released from a snare. "No longer am I captive," she murmured.

All about her the world felt safe. She could hear the mingled calls of birds, a rivulet of water falling over rocks, the softening of sound within the wooded shelter. The time had come for her to continue her journey yet she lay a moment longer, drinking in the beauty around her. Suddenly another sound caught her ear and Mara froze, the moment of peace replaced with panic.

Distant voices! Such fear filled her that she found herself unable to move, even knowing they neared. Instead she pressed her back close against the fallen log, lying still. Her arms felt like lead and were hardly able to reach out and grab the bundle from view, pressing the wet satchel to her chest. Her eyes shut tight, she forced herself to breath slowly so no sound escaped her lips. Mara could only hope that the thick fronds of forest plants and the heavy log hid her well enough to go without notice.

Wondering who walked through the forest, Mara strained her ears to catch the words. In a moment relief flooded her that these men were not Lamanites, but of her own kind. Still, what would they do if they found her? Having gone against the will of King Limhi, would she be slain? Suddenly she recognized a voice that she hadn't heard for several seasons. It was her grandfather's friend, the Nephite captain Gideon!

His voice was resolute. "Do each of you understand what must be done? Once we move closer to the fields we will be able to watch, and listen for the signal. Then we will fall upon the Lamanites and slay them. We are few, but it is our children and our wives and mothers whose lives we fight for."

A murmur of assent passed among the men and Mara, listening, felt bewildered. These soldiers didn't search for her, but instead prepared for war! What had happened that the Lamanites again fought with the Nephites?

"'Tis so, Gideon! We will fight for life, and fight unto death," one man said.

"We will fight with the fierceness of dragons!"

"It is good then," Gideon soberly answered. "Now let us travel northward for a short space, and prepare to meet our enemy."

"Are you sure they will come?" another asked.

"Yes. King Limhi observed the people of Laman from his tower, readying themselves in great numbers to destroy us.* They were at the place of arms, preparing weapons. It is likely that they will pass through these forests and fields, where many others of our warriors are now hiding. You are the last. Now, travel north to the place I have spoken of."

"Will you return to the king?"

"Yes, for my place is at his side in battle. We will be at the fore if I can reach him before the battle starts."

No more words were spoken. The men turned north-
* Mosiah 20:7-9

ward, passing closely by the place where Mara lay hidden. Her heart hammered as she held still, her muscles aching for release. Long after the sound of their tread had diminished she still stayed beneath the log, fearful to rise. When she couldn't bear it any longer she stirred, her joints stiff from the damp clothing and hard ground.

Rising, she looked about the forest yet saw no sign of the Nephite soldiers. Catching up her small bundle she moved away from where they had passed, treading with all caution. Her mind raced over the words she had heard spoken. She thought of King Limhi's tower built atop a hill outside the city wall. Once when she was a child Mara had been to the top of the tower with her father, and remembered how she could see far across the land. Cumeni had shown her the distant shimmer of black on the horizon, a lake of volcanic glass. It was there that the obsidian was obtained for weaponry, and if King Limhi had seen the Lamanite soldiers at the place of war, then Gideon was right. They would pass through these very forests and fields in a straight line to the city of Nephi.

Mara increased her pace, moving with haste across fallen logs and through dense brush. She no longer trembled at the thought of what she might face, nor did she think about her worries in finding the people of Alma. Instead she was filled with great determination, believing that if she didn't escape the land of Nephi-Lehi she would be killed with the rest of the Nephites. Whatever caused the Lamanites to come to war against her people, this time they would be destroyed. She had seen her foe's killing hatred once and now she fled from it, more certain than ever about the course she had chosen.

Travel through the forest became difficult, sometimes nearly impossible. In one place a stream cut through the forest forming a deep, dangerous ravine. Mara traveled along its edge searching for a place to cross, unaware that this course turned her in a northward direction. The silence of the forest was suddenly shattered by the piercing wail of a conch shell and the call, repeated down the line, grew louder.

At the signal cries of attack echoed through the forest, followed by the clash of weapons. The din of war reached Mara's ears, filling her with frightening memories which made her run blindly. Yet no matter which direction she turned, still the death screams reached her. Branches tore at her hair and flesh and vines entangled her feet, causing her to fall. Bruised and scratched, still she struggled on, passing closely by a throng of warriors who fought furiously. Intense in the battle they didn't see her and she hurried past.

Winded, Mara stopped to gasp in ragged breaths, leaning against a tree. She tried to force herself to think calmly, to make sane decisions. Pressing her forehead against the rough bark of the tree she closed her eyes, trying to call to mind the edge of the forests as seen from the city wall. She peered up through the overhead branches at the snatches of sky, unable to decide if she traveled north or south.

Suddenly a stray arrow flashed by her, sinking deep into the trunk with a loud thwack. Mara cried out, turning and fleeing away from the place. All direction lost, she fled blindly. Yet within a few minutes she had stumbled into the very midst of the battle. She caught a glimpse of fields beyond the edge of the forest where hundreds of men fought, crushing the pale gold harvest and staining it crimson with their blood. In her flight she burst into a clearing where a Lamanite fiercely battled two Nephite soldiers. She stopped, paralyzed by what she saw, by whom she saw.

Zeram swung his huge black cimeter, slicing death blows before the first man could use his sling. The rage he felt still burned within him, causing him to destroy many even though he knew the Nephite soldiers bore the advantage because of their surprise attack. He spun, facing the second who sought to use his short blade. The man made no cry when Zeram cut him down.

He swiftly turned to face the movement seen from the corner of his eye, his cimeter raised for death. Stunned, he faced Mara. Her eyes were wild like that of a doe stalked by a hunter. The soft flesh of her face was scratched, her tunic filthy, her hair damp and tangled. Zeram didn't know what to think. Why would a woman come to this place of battle? Why was this woman here!

There was no pause to question for she turned, fleeing from him in terror. He pursued, not given to reason or thought of the battle. With smooth glides he paced himself, spanning the distance between them. His cimeter was a burden yet he wouldn't drop it. Instead he forced himself to great speed, surging breaths moving in steady rhythm from his body, filling his ears.

Mara fled, unable to reason the direction. She could hear the Lamanite behind her, could feel his presence like a heat at her back. Sane thought would have turned her in another direction, yet she didn't have time to think. When her lungs were filled to bursting, the muscles in her legs knotted, she reached a crevice.

The forest floor fell away, the rivulet having widened into a small river far below. The cliff sides were deathly steep and Mara stared down into the depths. The Lamanite reached her, halting a span away. In his hands were blades of obsidian, stained scarlet with the blood of her people. She glanced back at the rocky crevice, not knowing how she would die. Then she turned, facing the warrior, her eyes dark with fear. They stood in silence, the sound of their gasping breaths harsh against the muffled quiet of the forest.

"You have come to kill," Mara said at last, her voice low. She faced him, willing her hands not to tremble, making them into fists.

Zeram neared, his manner deceptively calm, still the weapon was between them. "I have come to kill," he acknowledged. "But I have not come to kill you."

He reached out, grabbing hold of her arm and pulling her away from the edge of the ravine. She cried out, terrified. He looked down into her face. "Why are you here?"

Mara turned her head away, refusing to look at him. Could she once again ask him for mercy?

Another sound caught Zeram's attention and he looked up to see a Nephite soldier. The man was solid, scarred by many battles. "Lamanite, release the maiden!" he commanded.

"Gideon!" Mara cried.

The Nephite lunged at Zeram, grabbing his cimeter arm with all his strength. Having broken his blade in battle, Gideon had no weapon and his arrows were spent. Although Zeram was armed, Gideon was too close for Zeram to use the blade and Gideon forced the cimeter to the ground.

"Mara!" Gideon cried. "Flee!"

The two men grappled on the ground, striking each other with heavy blows. Although Zeram was the larger warrior, Gideon still proved a formidable foe. Mara turned and fled back along the ravine and away from the cries of battle.

She ran until she reached a place where the sides of the ravine were not so steep nor the water swift. Scrambling down the side she crossed over, ignoring the sharp stones that scored her feet. On the other side she swiftly flew across the dark forest floor and deep into the brush. When she could go no further she sank down, finding herself in a quiet place. No sound of war reached her, only the murmur of water running over moss-smooth stones.

Mara wept in terror and exhaustion, the sound echoing against the quiet of the woods.

Slowly Zeram opened his eyes, staring up at the trees and sky overhead. The sound of rushing water roared in his ears, his side numb from the cold. Not immediately understanding where he was, Zeram stirred, grimacing at the discomfort it brought. Forcing himself to sit up he glanced at the high edge of the ravine, then at the rushing water and sharp rocks he had fallen to. He flexed the stiff arm that had lain in the water, wondering where his cimeter was.

There was no sign of the Nephite soldier he had fought. The two had grappled near the edge of the ravine, and when the floor gave way Zeram had fallen to the base of the crevice, while the other gained a hand hold and pulled himself up. Why had his enemy not finished the task as Zeram lay unconscious by the side of the river? Had the soldier left him for dead?

Zeram stood, ignoring the pain where sharp stones had cut his back and head. Instead he grabbed hold of a thick root growing from the side of the ravine, pulling himself up the incline. When he reached the top he lay still, catching his breath and watching for signs of his enemy. Not far from him lay the cimeter where he had dropped it. Hastily he picked it up, striding through the forest. He berated himself for having left the battle to pursue the maiden, and yet the mystery of her presence still plagued him. Was he never to fight a battle that she did not cause to end? What was he to make of her, and the strange omen of her presence?

In a short span of time he found himself out of the forest and at the edge of the Nephite fields, yet to his dismay the battle was over. The fields lay littered with dead and Zeram withdrew into the shelter of trees, traveling with all haste back to his people. Coming over the edge of a small rise he could see the huge throng of Lamanite soldiers charging once again towards the city of Nephi. His heart lifted upon seeing they had regrouped and he joined them.

"Zeram!" Tholar called. "I thought you dead when you were not leading our plans."

"Only left for dead," he answered grimly. "Did our enemy drive us back?"

"Yes. They fought with great desperation, though they are few against our numbers. Do you know of King Laman, and how he has fallen?"*

Zeram stared at the other, forcing himself to keep pace as they marched. He could find nothing to say, instead he turned his eyes to the city.

Soon they marched upon the city of Nephi, ready to attack their enemy who spewed forth from the outer wall. The Lamanites, in the stance of war, stared at their foe in sudden silence. For the people came forth carrying no arms, and in their lead was the Lamanite ruler himself, King Laman. His wounds were bound, yet he could barely stand, aided on either side by two Nephite soldiers. King Laman bowed before his men. "My courageous warriors," he pleaded to everyone's astonishment, "listen to the words of the Nephites. They have words of great import to tell."

Not knowing what to think, the warriors lowered their weapons. King Limhi and his people came forward, telling the truth of what had happened to the Lamanite daughters. Gideon, the king's captain, came forward and spoke openly. Zeram stared in amazement because he recognized him. This was the man who had fought him for Mara's sake, who had left him at the bottom of the ravine and had not shed his blood.

* Mosiah 20:10-13

Gideon told of wicked priests his people had sought to destroy, who surely were the ones that had stolen the maidens. Zeram felt the weight of the moment, accepting the grim truth of what had happened to his sister. Hope of saving her began to fade as he listened to the words of the Nephites.

"We would ask you to forbear, that you lay not this thing to our charge," King Limhi pleaded.

King Laman stood, facing his men. "They have fulfilled the oath made to us. Shall we turn away from the oath I swore not to destroy them? Would they have come before you without arms, if this were not so?"*

The Lamanites soldiers studied the unarmed families, warily at first, and then slowly, one by one, they lowered their cimeters as their anger softened. Zeram looked around at the other soldiers. Would they yield so easily? He wanted to strike the Nephites down, to kill every soldier here and search their city for his sister. Yet even as these thoughts came he knew this was not the answer. Despite his anger Zeram knew enough of recent events among the Nephites to see that it could only be King Noah's priests who would be desperate enough to risk such a thing. Because of this he had no choice but to be obedient to King Laman's decree. Defeated, Zeram lowered his cimeter.

Seeing that continued warfare had been averted King Laman spoke quietly to Limhi. "I have kept my vow."

Limhi nodded. "We will send soldiers to search for Amulon and the others. Perhaps we will find them."

Laman was silent for a while. "It will be a hard thing for my people to forget the loss of our daughters," he stated, then rejoined his warriors. Silently the soldiers returned with their king to their own land.

* Mosiah 20:14-26

Zeram filled the net satchel with provisions, silently performing the task while some of the other Lamanites looked on. Finally Tholar spoke.

"Why do you do this, Zeram? Did you not believe the words of the Nephite captain and our king?"

"I believe them."

"Then how can you hope to find Saphira and the others, when even the Nephites do not know where their priests have gone?"

He looked up, his eyes angry. "What would you have me do? I cannot sit in the land of Shemlon, mourning our loss."

"King Laman commanded that we should stay," Tholar reminded him.

"I do not listen to a king who kneels before our foe, pleading their cause to save his own life," Zeram growled, tying the ends of the net. "Instead I seek for that which has been stolen, and to slay those who have done this thing. Who among you has the courage to join me?"

The other men looked away until Tholar spoke. "There can be no hope in such a scheme. What do you know of the wilderness which lies beyond the Nephite border? Not only will you never find the maidens, you will become lost if you journey into the deep forests."

"Am I the only one among you with courage?" Zeram sneered. When the others didn't look at him he picked up the satchel, slinging it across his shoulder and turning on his heel.

"There is no hope in such a plan," Corom murmured. "He takes the course of a fool."

"Zeram!" Tholar called after his friend, but Zeram did not look back. Instead he left the Lamanite camp, walking away from his people to seek and destroy the true Nephite thieves.

CHAPTER SIX

Saphira moved away from the edge of the fire, walking over to the place where some of her sister Lamanites sat. Behind them the sky was streaked with the colors of flame, another day dying. She knelt down beside the others who silently watched the men prepare the camp for the evening. How many days had passed, she wondered? Their trek had been long, exhaustion making one day fade into the next.

She bent near her sisters, her eyes catching their attention. "The men grow careless," she murmured. "Let us try to flee tonight while they sleep."

The others stared at her until Hathomi spoke. "Do you talk of escape?"

"Yes," she answered, her voice barely audible.

"How could we find our way?" Hathomi whispered. "We do not know where our homeland is from this place, and the forests were great that we traveled through."

"I have counted the rivers we crossed," Saphira answered. "Three narrow, one wide, ten and two narrow. Our kinsmen are only ten and six rivers away, and even now they are surely searching for us. Tonight I flee. Who will go with me?"

Many of the others looked away, then one called Zoaph spoke, her voice filled with sadness. "I cannot return to our people, for how shall I enter into the house of my father when I am no longer a maiden?"

Saphira stared at her, stunned.

"Zoaph speaks the truth," Hathomi said, bowing her head

in shame. "How can we return home? Once defiled we can do nothing but stay with these men and be their women."

"Is it so with all of you?" Saphira choked.

The others gave a slight nod, then questioned her with their eyes until she made the sign of disavowal. Zoaph looked over at the one called Samuel, then she turned back to Saphira. "Has the younger one left you untouched?"

"Yes," Saphira whispered.

"Then take leave tonight," Zoaph said, reaching out and grabbing Saphira's arm. Her grip tightened. "Flee before it is too late."

Saphira put her hand to her eyes, the sudden wetness there stinging. "And what of you?" she finally asked, the ache of sorrow hard within her.

Hathomi touched her. "Heshlon has said we will soon dwell in a valley, living as husband and wife, and that I must bear him sons. So it will be that we do the part of woman, except that it shall be with these men instead of our own kin."*

Saphira said nothing further, her heart heavy. One of the men entered the camp dragging a kill, commanding the women to clean and prepare the meat. She stood, blindly following through the task with the others. They skinned the deer and sliced up the hind quarters, tossing the meat into the fire where it filled the air with smoke.

The night had grown late when Saphira finally lay down on the skin pallet, tired from the task of preparing the meat. Sleep threatened her yet she forced herself to stay awake, and when the fire finally burned low, a shallow glow of red against the blackness of night, she merely pretended to sleep. Samuel took his place beside her and soon she could hear his slow breathing. One thing became more apparent to her than ever. Samuel the Nephite was different from the others. He had shown her kindness in a setting of cruelty.

* Mosiah 23:33-34

Overhead the moon shone round and bright, filling Saphira with awe as it had so often in the past. She didn't understand its trek nor the strange faces it wore, yet tonight in its full form it would help guide her way. Much time passed and still she waited until the embers of the fire were nearly extinguished and the moon had traveled halfway across the sky.

Believing all to be asleep she slowly knelt, crouching low. She studied Samuel, then cautiously moved away from him, crawling along the ground and past others deep in slumber. Saphira didn't know that there was one who watched.

Sleep had eluded Jubal, who sorely felt the anger of his loss made sharper as time had worn on. Over the past days he had watched the Lamanite maiden taken from him, his eyes constantly studying the manner in which her black hair fell about her face, and how she moved with grace. He believed her to be more fair than any of the others and his desire for her grew. He spent his time filled with bitter resentment, staring at the place where she lay beside Samuel. Suddenly he detected a movement which he didn't understand at first, his eyes straining through the darkness. When the form passed through a shaft of pale moonlight he realized what was happening. Jubal grinned to himself, feeling for the knife secure within his belt. He had known that if he were patient the maiden would again be his.

He rose to his feet, a plan quickly forming in his mind. He would slay the young fool while he slept, and then pursue the maiden. When he brought her back all would believe it was she who had slain her captor. She would be given into his care, and his despised foe would be destroyed just as Jubal had so often dreamed!

Saphira reached the edge of the camp and stood, ready to flee into the forest. Her heart raced with fear as she turned to look back, hoping no one had detected her. At first she saw nothing, and then a movement caught her eye and she froze. She could barely make out the form of a man who crouched low, moving among the others. She had been seen! The startled thought made her want to turn and flee, yet reason made her wait a moment longer. If the Nephite had seen her, why hadn't he cried out? The gray outline of the man passed near the coals of the fire and her heart turned to stone, a shudder of fear gripping her. She needn't see the man's small, cruel eyes nor his sneer of contempt to recognize him. She could tell from the outline of his girth that it was Jubal, and that he was ready to pounce on the younger man who lay sleeping.

A terrible decision pulled at her, threatening to rend her in two. Samuel's life, or her freedom? Saphira clenched her fists, then made her decision.

At her shout of warning, Samuel jolted awake and rolled to the side, barely moving out of the way as a heavy figure lunged at him. In a moment he was grabbing the attacker's arm, pushing it up to keep the knife from slicing into his throat. He was aware of the terrible threat, of Jubal's hot breath in his face, and of his own arms shuddering under the weight of the other. They were grappling, struggling against one another, the knife between them. The blood pounded in Samuel's head as he fought his opponent. There was no time to think, only the instinctual movements of survival. The knife sliced down and he twisted to the side, feeling the blade brush by his neck and sink into the earth.

Both their hands were on the hilt now, slick with sweat, as Jubal jerked the blade from the earth. Samuel used his feet and legs to push up, dislodging his opponent's weight. The two rolled on the ground, Jubal grunting when Samuel's elbow caught him in the ribs. The heavy man's fist hit the side of his head but the younger man gritted his teeth, knowing he must not let go of the knife. In a last desperate movement Samuel grabbed Jubal's hand, shoving it up and away from him, feeling a sickening pressure as he heard the man's scream. Samuel rolled free, lying on his back and gasping for air.

Aware of blood on his own chest and the moans of his opponent, Samuel stared stunned at Jubal before looking at the men who had gathered around. He sat up, facing them. Amulon stepped near, shoving the heavy man with his foot to turn him over. Jubal gave a scream of pain and they all stared at the knife sticking into his belly.

"Son, are you harmed?" Heshlon cried. He gave Samuel his hand, helping him to his feet.

"No, Father," Samuel answered, still amazed by what had happened. "I slept, and he attacked. If it were not for the warning. . . ."

He looked about the camp. Where was Saphira? Amulon answered his unspoken question. "Your woman has fled back into the forest. We will look for her."

"Wait," Samuel said. "I will go alone to find her."

"Let us help you," Heshlon said. "You cannot find her by yourself."

"She has not gone far. It was her fear of Jubal which made her flee," he answered, trying to convince Amulon and the others.

"Many searchers are better than one," Amulon said.

"She is my woman, and I will find her." His voice was firm and as the others stared down at Jubal, twice defeated, no one could doubt Samuel had the right to make that choice.

He turned and headed in the direction he believed Saphira had taken, not wanting the others to follow.

Jubal began to moan, the pain crossing over him in waves. He opened his eyes, peering up at those around him, mouthing words of pleading. Amulon stared at him in disgust, then reached down and pulled out the blade. The Zoramite screamed and fainted.

"Will he die?" one asked.

"He is a coward. I care nothing whether he dies or lives," Amulon answered. The others walked away, but one taking pity on him bade his woman bind the wound.

Once in the forest Samuel didn't hurry, instead he listened and looked to see if he could detect where Saphira had gone. A cold sweat broke out on his chest and face, and he shuddered in the aftermath of his fight. He had come close to death. Pausing, he took in a slow, deep breath.

He knew it had been Saphira who had screamed his name, warning him. If she had kept silent and let Jubal do his wicked deed, she could have used the fight for cover and none would have noticed her escape. He wondered about this. He also wondered if he would be able to find her in the forest. If he could be sure she could safely travel back to her people he would even now return to camp, but they had come so far through the wilderness that he feared for her.

Saphira's cry had saved his life, and he realized she had warned him even though she owed him nothing. He had taken her from her people, dragged her into the wilderness, and still she had chosen to warn him.

Samuel thought over all that had happened and came to a decision. Through the past two years he had sorrowed over his foolish choices, and those of his people. Yet no longer did he wish to live with the knowledge of his misdeeds. He was helpless to make recompense for the actions of his brethren, but not so with the maiden given to him. If he found

Saphira he would right the wrong. He would repay the debt of her warning by returning her to her people.

The night had seemed unusually long to Saphira. Her feet ached where sharp twigs and rocks had scored them, and her entire being felt heavy with exhaustion, but still she pushed on. Again and again her mind replayed the scene of Jubal's attack on Samuel. She wondered if even now Samuel might lay dying, and the thought made her heart feel like a heavy stone.

She heard the sound of rushing water before she reached the steep ravine, and in the darkness she feared that crossing it would be dangerous. Instead she turned along it's edge, fighting her way through dense brush. How long she had traveled she couldn't guess, only knowing that the moon had disappeared from overhead. The forest seemed more darkly threatening than ever and she felt her way along with trepidation.

When she could go no further she sank down among a patch of blade brush, very disheartened. Her plan of escape had appeared so direct! She had counted the rivers. She knew that her homeland lay in a northward direction. Yet now, in the ominous surroundings of giant trees and thick undergrowth, Saphira realized her plan was foolish. Even warriors seeking other cities had been known to become lost in the wilderness. She was a lone woman, fleeing from her captors, with no food or even a weapon. Was it any wonder that the other maidens had stared at her in amazement when she spoke of escape?

Overcome with discouragement she closed her eyes, letting her tired legs rest. Soon she slept, yet only a short time had passed when she awakened. Realizing her situation she decided that the Nephites would certainly pursue her. It had been careless to rest. She forced herself up, stretching stiff muscles before traveling on. Eventually a gray light began to spread through the forest and she could see the dark water far below. The ravine was narrow but deathly steep, the water surging over jagged rocks. The river appeared larger than she had believed and the thought plagued her that she had gone in the wrong direction. What should she do? If she continued on, the river might become a torrent unable to be crossed, yet turning back was no solution since her captors might even now be close behind.

Saphira pushed forward, struggling through the vines that continually caught at her feet. The forest sounds echoed eerily about her and she shuddered. Hope suddenly filled her when she came to a place where an old, rotted tree had fallen across the ravine. Upon reaching it she examined the bark, unable to move it she concluded it would be safe to cross over.

Taking a deep breath she climbed on the log, her heart quickening within her when she looked down at the water and jagged rocks so far below. The fear of falling into the ravine made her unable to walk across. Instead she pulled up the hem of her shift, catching it into a knot at her waist. Then she knelt down, inching her way onto the tree. The rough bark scratched her palms and knees, yet determinedly she worked her way across.

Slowly she neared the middle of the ravine, her arms nearly shaking. Far below she could see the rush of water which moved with mighty force. The sight of its swift flow made her feel weak and she lifted her gaze, staring at the outline of the trees ahead.

All about her the gray light of early dawn began to take on a pearly hue, allowing her to more clearly make out the line of trees and bank. Trembling, she neared the end of the log, her heart triumphant. Certainly with the river between her and her captors, escape would be possible. With the coming of light they would more easily be able to find her, but once across the water she would flee into the forest and far away from them.

Samuel gazed up at the pale sky overhead which spoke of the coming of dawn. His tunic was soaked, his muscles aching from his most recent ordeal of having crossed the river. He had traveled in a direct line from the camp, assuming that in her haste Saphira would have done the same. When he reached the ravine he decided that she might have crossed it, the same as the group had done the day before. Yet he hadn't realized how difficult it would be in the darkness and without the aid of a rope and guide.

The torrent nearly drowned him, dragging him downstream and knocking him against boulders and rocks until he managed to reach the far embankment and pull himself out. If Saphira had been so foolish as to try and cross the river then she might have drowned. Yet if she didn't, then had she gone in some other direction?

He moved along, his heart heavy with discouragement. He believed that he stood no chance of finding her now, not among the dense trees and certainly not with the barrier of the river. Yet he couldn't turn back to the safety of the fire, to the place where his father stayed. The thought of doing so filled him with emptiness. And the thought of Saphira gone from him made his heart suddenly ache with a misery he couldn't explain.

Saphira, a maiden fair above all others, a woman strong in a time of travail, had been given to him by his leader. He wondered if he would ever see her again. Perhaps she would perish in the forest, a place of danger filled with wild beasts where no maiden should journey without protection. Yet if through some miracle she were to make her way back to the Lamanite land, what hope would there be? Certainly her kinsmen would seek his life, as was their right because of what he and the others had done.

Samuel forced himself to keep up the pace, traveling in the direction he hoped she had taken.

Trembling, Saphira slowly stood up amid the gnarled roots of the tree where they jutted into the air and entwined with the overhead branches of a giant cedar. She undid the hem of her tunic and let it fall, then turned back to look across the narrow way she had come. The magnitude of her actions filled her with pride and she smiled, pleased that she had overcome her fears. In the distance she saw pale red-gold light edge the embankment and the log she had crossed over. It seemed a token, an omen of success and her heart felt light.

Saphira turned back to her new course and her breath caught in her throat, a startled cry escaping her. Samuel!

"Saphira," he said in a low voice. The Nephite stood only a short span away, staring at her. His eyes assessed her, his countenance sober except for his quickened breath.

A moan of angry protest escaped her lips and she took a step back. How had he found her! Behind her the way had been greatly difficult. Could she cross back over with Samuel in pursuit? Fear and uncertainty filled her, and the only thing which kept her from fleeing back across the dangerous ravine was that he made no movement towards her.

She studied him for some sign, for the threat of what he and his kind were, and all the while her mind raced with the knowledge that he had found her. How had he come to stand before her when she only now crossed the river?

His expression did nothing to assure her, instead his face became one of alarm. "Come here now!" he commanded.

Saphira shook her head, moving back as he lunged towards her. Yet she had no moment for thought, instead a scream wrenched itself from her lips as a huge serpent dropped on her from the overhead branches. Its barred, hissing fangs were in her face when Samuel grabbed its throat, pulling back with all the strength in his fist. She shoved the slithering coil from around her neck, staggering away from the touch of the deadly serpent as Samuel cast it high into the air where it plummeted into the ravine.

Sobbing, she stood shaking, unable to move or think. Samuel hurried to her, grabbing her arms in his hands, looking at her to make sure she was unharmed. He felt helpless, seeing her weep, and before he knew how it had come about she was tight in his grasp. He held her shuddering form close within the warmth of his arms, saying soothing words. He stroked the tangled mass of black hair, aware of her frailty.

Until this moment she had never wept. He had seen only her strength, yet it was her weakness which filled him with tenderness.

The terror of the moment passed and Saphira managed to subdue her tears. She became intently aware of Samuel's arms about her, of the feel of his rough tunic beneath her cheek and the way he stroked her hair and murmured words of comfort. She forced the sobs back, pulling away and brushing at the wetness on her face. She wouldn't look at him.

Samuel quietly spoke. "There is no shame in your weeping."

Saphira finally lifted her eyes. "How did you find me?"

"I crossed the river and traveled along its edge. It was only chance that I saw you."

She sat down on part of the tree, dejection in the movement. "Where are the others?"

"I have come alone."

This statement surprised and disconcerted her. She didn't know what to think. "You will take me back, then?" she said at last.

Samuel sighed and sat down beside her. His hands felt empty as he looked at her. "No, I will not. Saphira, there is much I would speak." He struggled for the words. "I believe that what we did, stealing you and the other maidens, was wrong. My desire is to right that wrong, and the only thing I can do is to take you back to your people."

"You would do that?" she asked, her voice showing all the emotion she felt.

"Yes," he murmured.

"But the other men. . . ."

"They will not find us. The wilderness is great and after they search for a day they will give up hope."

"Can we find our way back to my homeland?" she asked.

"I do not know. We will try."

Another thought plagued her. "If my kinsmen find us they will slay you."

"Yes, yet I think that I can escape such a thing if we are watchful."

Saphira soberly thought this over. "Then what shall become of you, Samuel of the Nephites? You may never be able to find your way back to your father and the others. How shall I let you sacrifice yourself for my sake?"

"I can see no other way. Will you go back with me to my people, and be my woman?"

The question startled her, a flush of color heightening the dark silk of her cheeks. "If you ask me," she said at last. "If the choice is mine, I would not. I would not chose to live among your kind."

Samuel felt the weight of her words. "Come, then," he said, standing and taking her hand. She stood. "I see no decision, then, but to set about the course of returning you to your people."

His hand felt warm where it encircled hers as he led her over fallen logs and into the thickness of the forest where the light again became dim. All about them were shadows and the strange and eerie calls of wild fowl. They stopped once when he took time to break the stems from a long branch. He used this as a pole to push back the foliage and more easily allow them to pass.

They went on in silence, surrounded by the frightening beauty of the wilderness, isolated together in a sea of trees. Once they stopped at a stream to drink, and later assuaged their hunger with the fruit growing on a wild neas vine. The sun stood high overhead when they finally rested, and Saphira sat across from Samuel, studying him.

"I feared you had died," she said.

"Jubal tried to kill me, but he fell on his own knife during our fight and I do not know if he still lives. If you had not screamed a warning, he would have succeeded in his intent. Did your fear of his attack make you flee?"

She looked away. "No, it was my plan to escape. I had nearly done so when I looked back and saw him ready to attack you."

Samuel thought about this. "If you had not cried out you could have freely escaped."

"Yes, I know. But then I would have sacrificed your life in the place of my freedom."

"I owe you my life, then," he answered soberly.

A smile touched her lips and he returned it.

"You have cause for merriment?" he asked, to hide the feelings foreign to him.

"Not merriment," she answered. "But happiness, yes. You cannot know how my heart turned to stone at seeing you standing before me. I felt such fear, and yet you not only saved me from the serpent but will lead me home. My heart can feel nothing but joy, Samuel of the Nephites."

He smiled and shook his head. "Perhaps your joy would not be so full if you knew how lost I am. It seems of little good that I seek to return you home, when every way we travel is strange to me."

Saphira grew thoughtful. "I do not mind that we are lost, since at least we are lost together."

Samuel suddenly laughed, the sound startling a pair of wild doves in the branches overhead.

"Now is it you who has cause for merriment?" Saphira asked.

"Yes. For the first time I do that which is right, not what I have been told to do. Also I have found you when I thought you would be lost to me forever. My heart feels merry, even though reason would make me have more sense about the plight we are in."

Saphira smiled again, her own heart light. "Then let us go," she said, standing. "I want to be far from your people before nightfall."

Samuel stood, catching up his staff and leading the way.

Darkness spread its eagle wings across the land, sending out low shadows until the scape lay covered. Overhead the stars stood out, bright and scattered crystals on a black sky. The two sat beneath a gnarled cedar, a small fire smoldering between them. Sparks of red floated up, the flames dancing on the wood in colors of heat.

Samuel turned the spit, roasting the fowl he had snared and which Saphira had plucked. The grease from it dripped into the fire, hissing and sputtering, its aroma adding to their hunger. Saphira stared into the flames. "I could eat the bird nearly raw," she said at last, causing Samuel to laugh.

"I think it is done enough," he said, lifting the meat from the fire and placing it on a mat of leaves. He waited only a few moments for it to cool before pulling out his small knife and cutting off pieces of the breast. He handed her some of the meat, eating also. Saphira ate the unseasoned fowl, thinking that no food since the time of her captivity had tasted so good.

When their hunger had ebbed and they had stripped the last of the meat to eat on the morrow, the fire burned low. Satisfied, Samuel leaned back against the cedar, studying Saphira.

"In all my memory I cannot recall one as fair as you, Saphira. You are well named, for your hair wears the gems of the fire. Even now the light of it lines your face in such a way that I think I shall always remember this night. You are a rare maiden, one whose worth is far above gold or silver."

She felt his words and the intensity of his voice, wondering if he could see her face gain color in the dim light from the fire. "No man has spoken to me thus," she said at last, the words feeling awkward.

"Do you disdain my saying such things?"

Saphira took in a slow breath. "No, for how shall I disdain one who has spared me?"

"How have I spared you?"

Silence grew thick between them and she forced herself to answer. "The others of your kind have defiled my sisters."

She turned her face aside and Samuel didn't speak for a while. Instead he studied the fire, watching it die down into white coated embers.

"I have spent much time studying you, Saphira," he said at last. "It has been many seasons since I have even been in the presence of a woman, any woman. Then to have been entrusted with one such as yourself . . . you cannot know how I have desired you. And yet my desire is not as that of my brethren. For that which I feel for you is of a great tenderness."

He paused and Saphira turned to intently watch him, studying the way shadows cast by the fire edged the lines of his face. He sighed and shook his head as if to clear it. "It would be my greatest pleasure to take you as my woman, but I know one thing. You would not be mine for the taking until the time that you came to me of your own choice."

He said nothing more and she marveled at all he had spoken, unable to answer him. At last he stood. "Come, lie beside the fire. At first light we must travel in the direction of your homeland."

Saphira did as he bade, laying beside the warmth of the embers and closing her eyes. Sleep half wound itself about her when she became aware of his presence close behind her, as it had so often been in the past. "Samuel?" she murmured.

"What is it?"

"Do you remember when you asked if I would be willing to join your people?"

"Yes, Saphira, I remember."

"What would you answer me if I were to ask the same thing of you? What would you say if I asked you to join my people?"

The reply was long in coming. "I would answer no," he said at last. "It could never be."

Saphira was so quiet that he felt certain she simply slept and had not heard his answer, until she spoke. "If I will not join your kind, and be your woman, and you will not join my kin and be my kinsman, then you and I shall never be. There is no place for us."

He felt her voice, full with sorrow, and his own soul echoed back its answer even as he held his peace.

CHAPTER SEVEN

The Waters of Mormon lay like a shimmering blue jewel, its clear depths reflecting the jagged mountains surrounding it. In the far distance a narrow waterfall split the stone face of layered cliffs, disappearing into the jungle. Among the descendants of Lehi there was great reverence for the sacred places of water and holy mountains. This lake was a place of peace. The quiet air, the depth of sky reflected in water, the mountains draped in mists, all spoke of peace.

Mara walked along the bank, her heart calm in the quiet serenity of a sacred place. The memories of war and captivity seemed to fade from her, leaving her free of that which had plagued her for so long now. And yet, despite the calm she felt, her heart was heavy. For here, in this most quiet and beautiful place, she was alone. There were no followers of Alma, no people who believed as her mentor had once believed. They were gone. She had tarried too long in fulfilling her promise, and now when she finally reached the place Riplah had spoken of, she was too late.*

For the first time Mara didn't know what to do. She had escaped the city, had seen a war set upon her people, and then traveled through the wilderness to reach this place. Yet now that she had come to her destination she felt lost. There would be no returning to the city of Nephi, for certainly the Lamanites must have destroyed her land. No matter how Gideon and the others fought, they were few against the fierce numbers of their adversaries. Yet even if Mara could have

* Mosiah 23:1-2

turned back, she didn't want to. Being here, in this sacred place, made her remember the teachings of her mother's father and those quiet whisperings she had only begun to feel.

In time she reached a site where many people had once been. She saw small rings of stone where fires had burned, yet from the tares that grew around them she knew much time must have passed since the people of Alma had come here. Near the shore was a large, round stone once used as an altar, and she approached it, touching its cold surface. The bittersweet resin of incense still remained on its surface signifying sacred rites once performed. The people of Alma had been here, and this was their place of worship.

Looking about Mara spied an outcropping of wild neas and hastily gathered the dark green fruit. The cheese and corn in her bundle were long since eaten and hunger made her anxious. She sat down on a stone near the altar, peeling off the rough skin to reveal the soft, oily meat of the neas which had become her ancestor's substitute for the olive. She ate all of the pale green center down to the smooth egg shaped pit, casting it aside. The other fruits she put in her bundle, knowing hunger would come again soon enough.

Then Mara began to ponder what she should do. Beside the quiet lapping of water the distant song of a quetzal bird echoed across the waves, and she drank in the peace of the place. Her mind turned to a happier time when she had knelt with Riplah. Many times since her captivity she had prayed for help, remembering the words which he had taught her. Yet now she felt such desperation and need that she found herself kneeling at the altar with an intensity unlike anything before.

Mara prayed aloud, her words strange in the quiet, and yet she didn't cease. How long she knelt in supplication was uncertain yet when she finally lifted up her eyes it seemed much time had passed. It also seemed that she was no closer to an answer than before, even though the worries in her heart had eased. In despair she laid her head against the stone, her palm sliding down the side of the altar. Unknowingly her fingers brushed along a strange shape and she sat up to look at what she had touched. Near the base of the altar, hidden by plant blades, was an engraving.

She gasped and her fingers anxiously tracing over the lines and shape that had been carved into the stone. The pattern was small, nearly the size of her palm, and depicted a form well known to her. Quickly she grabbed the cord around her neck and pulled up the golden glyph. She snatched it off, laying it against the altar to compare the two. They were the same, the simple pattern of a tree carved in relief.

Riplah's words came back to her and she remembered the day he had given it. "This is a symbol to the followers of Christ, to those who study the teachings of Abinadi and of Alma."

Mara stared at the two shapes, the tiny gold glyph and the larger stone carving, nearly the same. The only difference was in the coloring. Hers was light, the other had been partially covered in dark resin, making more than half of it black. She sat for a long time studying the carving, thoughtfully tracing its shape with her fingers. Why the dye upon the stone? What did it signify?

The answer, slow in coming, filled her with awe at the sudden understanding. Black! Wasn't it the color representing North? Among the traditions of her people the north was a land of darkness, symbolized by the color black, even as red was the color for south. The people of Alma had traveled away from the city of Nephi, but in a northward direction, not south. She gazed up at the ridge of land leading away from the waters, heading north, and suddenly she felt sure of what to do.

Mara's heart filled with hope even though she knew traveling through the mountain wilderness would be a difficult task. Yet hadn't the Great One answered her prayer, even this very hour? If she had been shown the glyph in the stone, certainly she would be shown the way. On the morrow she would set out, traveling along the ridge leading across the mountains and away from the Waters of Mormon. She smiled to herself, then began to sing the high, sweet strains of a song she had known from childhood.

When the forest broke on the water's edge, Zeram stared in awe at the scene before him. The sun sank behind misted mountains, spreading gold across the smooth expanse of water, darkness at its edge in the shadow of the cliffs. He immediately went to the bank and threw himself on his belly, scooping the cool water into his mouth to ease his thirst. His water bag had long since been empty and he eagerly drank. When he had slaked his thirst he stood, again studying the glorious scene and wondering how he had managed to find such a place.

He had wandered several days in the forests, only happening on this place when he had nearly despaired. When he left the valley in Shemlon it was not long before he lost the trail of the maidens and their captors, wandering in a direction he was unsure of. Even now he feared that the words of the others were true, and that no man could find them. He had little hope of saving Saphira and the others, for the trail was cold and he had wandered far through an unknown land. Yet now, reaching this place of clear water, his spirits lifted.

He ate the last of the meat he carried, deciding that at first light he would spear fish. Yet now exhaustion overtook him and he lay down on some ferns, closing his eyes as darkness settled on the land.

When Zeram woke he could see the stars through the

overhead branches and he listened to the night rustlings of the forest and the lapping water. Sleep left him and he sat up, stretching. He stared out over the black water when something caught his attention. A glimmer of gold on the edge of the water, a tiny flicker, held his gaze. Slowly he stood, his muscles growing tense as he realized that a fire burned on the distant shore.

He quickly caught up his satchel and spear, moving along the bank. In the darkness it was difficult to travel and yet he hurried, always keeping his eyes on the glint of light. Someone was on the far side of the water and had built a fire. With each step he took he felt more certain than ever that it was those he sought.

The night grew strange, for no matter how far he walked the light seemed to always stay the same, beckoning yet ever elusive. The wind from off the water touched his bare arms and chest, chilling him. Night hunters stalked the skies, dipping low across the glassy surface of the water, while overhead the expanse of stars and sky were reflected in the dark abyss. For a moment he lost sight of the fire among the trees, hastening all the more. Then he nearly stumbled into the small clearing in his eagerness to find it again. Quickly he pulled back.

Zeram crouched down to study the scene. Every sense was aware, warning him lest there was a trap, for he saw no men or people. Only a fire built by a large rock, and a lone form lying beside it. He tried to still his breath, his ears straining for any sound, yet after a few moments he came to believe that there were no others. He would have heard feet moving through the brush or in the branches overhead. Instead all he heard was the soft wind from the water and the low crackle of burning embers.

He studied the form lying beside the fire, easily discerning that it was a woman. He saw the red glow edge the line of hip and arm, the head covered by a shawl, and his heart leapt within him. Saphira?

He moved toward her, setting down his spear and kneeling beside the sleeping form. His hand gently touched her arm and he called her name. The maiden stirred, turning to look up at him and he sat back on his heels in shocked amazement.

Mara screamed, scurrying away from the Lamanite. She had no thought except terror at being found, at the evil dream which had taken form. Not quick enough to escape, he grabbed her, pulling her back to the fire. He held her near the flames, letting the light edge her features.

Zeram couldn't speak or think. All he could do was stare down into the face of the Nephite maiden. Stunned, he did nothing as she railed at him, striking out with her fists on his face and chest. She continued to reign blows on him until he caught her hands, pulling them down.

"Why have you come for me?" she sobbed. "I will not return with you! I will not go back!"

He continued to say nothing, only holding her captive, watching the emotions play across her face. He couldn't fathom why she was here until he thought about the time he had most recently seen her in the forest. She had been fleeing her land. When the Nephite captain attacked him she had escaped into the forest, and this was the place she had come to. Once he understood this Zeram let her go, though his eyes still held her captive.

Mara took in a ragged, startled breath at his release. She wiped away the wetness on her cheeks, staring at him in apprehension. "How have you found me?" she choked, her eyes accusing.

"I was not looking for you," he answered, his own voice harsh.

Mara stared at him, uncertain. "Then why are you here?"

"I seek my sister, stolen by your people."

His words echoed into the quiet, silence thickening between them.

"I do not understand," she said at last, hesitant. "You warred against our city, no doubt your men have destroyed all those in the land of Nephi, and now you say this."

"Your city, and those within it, are not destroyed. We left them in peace."

"I saw the battle! Would you have me believe such words?" she skeptically asked.

He scowled, sitting down cross-legged by the fire. A band of leather tied across his brow pulled back his black hair, and beside him was a spear and satchel. His appearance seemed forbidding despite his casual posture, his dark eyes studying her. "I never lie. I am not like the Nephites."

The words stung her. "Neither do I lie," she stated, knowing that now both would be bound to speak only the truth. "Why did you attack our city?"

Zeram didn't immediately answer, the flickering amber light playing shadows across the angles of his face. "My sister, Saphira, was the only daughter of our father and mother, I the only son. Many seasons ago our parents went the way of all the earth, and we share the single bond of kin."

He took in a slow breath before continuing, then looked up at the sky overhead. "Saphira and the other maidens went to a place to make merry, and while there men came upon them and carried them away. There were twenty and four maidens, and the men were Nephites."

Mara felt stunned. "Can you be so sure?" she asked at last.

"We made war on your people, believing they had done this thing. Yet when King Laman fell into the hands of your King Limhi, he persuaded our leader to plead his cause. Limhi and your people came before us without arms to cry for mercy and swear their innocence."

Mara thought about all he told her. "Did you believe them?"

"I believe it was not men from the city of Nephi who did this thing, but Nephites still the same. One of your captains, the same one who attacked me for your sake, spoke on behalf of your people. He said that it was the remnant of King Noah's priests."

Mara took in a startled breath and Zeram closely studied her. "Can Gideon be right?" she finally asked.

"I think he spoke the truth in this one thing." Zeram was aware of how she bent her head, her very posture taking on the position of sorrow.

"Why do you mourn the fate of the Lamanite maidens?" he asked at last.

"Because if this is true, then one of those who did this thing was once my father," she whispered.

Zeram grimly sat back, putting together all the things he could remember about Mara. "Yes," he said at last. "I had not remembered until now that your father was one of the king's priests."

"He is not my father," she said defiantly. "He ceased to be my father when he followed King Noah and abandoned his people."

"And abandoned you?"

Mara said nothing, instead she leaned dejectedly against the large stone, wrapping her arms about her knees.

"Now," he said, squarely facing her. "I have told the truth in all things. And you have said you do not lie."

Mara realized the challenge. He expected her to explain her presence here. She took in a slow breath. "Lamanite, you have been the enemy of my people for too long. If I speak of myself, what safety is there in this? How shall I know that you will not force me to return

captive to the city? I will not go back," she said with bitter force.

"Why? Is it not your home?" he asked, puzzled.

"What is home? Is it a place where I must dwell captive?
A place that every day reminds me of what my people once
were, and what their cowardice has brought them?"

Zeram suddenly laughed, the sound strange in the night
silence. "You speak like a man," he said. "I have never met a
maiden such as yourself. How did you escape the city when
Nephite guards stand watch on the city walls and our soldiers watch the borders of your land?"

"I left the city through the water causeway where the
soldiers on the wall would have difficulty seeing below. I
also studied the places of your guards from the city wall, but
could not see them once I reached the fields. Now I know it
is because they had gone to the place of weapons to join the
rest of your warriors."

He thought this over. "Did you escape because you knew
from the Nephite captain that we planned an attacked?"

"I knew nothing of the battle until I chanced on it in
the forest."

"Then you planned to escape before," he stated, his voice
thoughtful.

Mara felt uncertain, fearful that she had said too much.
She looked away but still he questioned her.

"Why?" He demanded. When she didn't answer he
leaned near, peering into her face. "You said you do
not lie."

"I do not lie," she repeated. "But I would not tell you
this thing, so I say nothing."

He scowled at her. "You escape to seek your father and
the other priests."

"Lamanite," she hissed. "Have you listened to nothing I

have said? Cumeni is no longer my father. He is dead to me. Would I leave the city to seek the dead?"

Slowly he shook his head. "Yet I know you seek something."

They studied each other in the dying glow from the fire. At last he tossed his things aside, moving to lay next to the warmth of the embers. "You had best sleep," he said over his shoulder.

Mara didn't know what to think. It appeared he wouldn't take her captive, although she felt that if she were to try and escape he could easily find her. She moved to the other side of the fire, lying down and staring at his back.

"Lamanite?" she asked. "Where do you travel from here?"

"I do not know," he answered, his voice muffled. Then when she thought he would say nothing more, "I am called Zeram."

Mara stared into the darkness. She had forgotten his name, and now that he had spoken it there seemed less to fear. Perhaps tomorrow at first light she could slip away while he still slept, and travel to the place northward.

Closing her eyes, sleep came.

Early morning light shimmered on the water, its surface like a thousand opals catching glints of blue and green and white. Zeram stood at its edge, studying the expanse before him. For a reason he could not explain he felt at peace for the first time in many seasons. He wondered if this were a sacred place, and what it meant that he should have found the Nephite maiden here. He walked down the bank and then waded into the water at a shallow place that formed a ledge. He could see silver fish darting quickly past and he held still, ignoring the cold water and the sharp stones beneath his feet. If he were patient the fish could be speared.

Mara's eyes were closed and she listened to the lapping of the water and the songs of the morning birds. When she remembered her meeting with the Lamanite she opened her eyes. She saw that he was gone although fuel had been added to the coals and a small fire burned. She quickly sat up, spying him a short distance away. Zeram—she recalled his name—stood thigh deep in the water, his spear poised. She watched in fascination as he brought the lance down with a quick stab and brought it back up, a speared fish flopping back and forth. He tossed the fish on the ground and turned back into his frozen stance, staring down at the water. Some time passed before he jabbed the spear in again and brought it up empty. Three more tries and then another fish writhed on the point.

Zeram brought the two fish back to the fire, tossing them on the coals. Then he sat down across from Mara. She stared into the fire, regretting that she had failed to slip away. Uncertain in his presence, she didn't know what to do.

The fish stopped moving, smoke rising up from the fire while they cooked. "I thought you would have fled during the night," Zeram said aloud.

Startled, Mara looked up at him. "I slept too long," she finally answered.

Zeram gave a short laugh, but when Mara said nothing more they sat in silence, watching the fire. When the fish had charred on one side he turned them with a stick. "How did you find this place?" he asked.

"My grandfather taught me of it."

"And why have you come here?"

Mara didn't know how to answer him. It wasn't in her to lie, neither did she wish to try and evade his questioning any more. She took in a slow breath. "This is a sacred place."

"Yes, I know it."

She questioned him with her eyes and he pointed to the

water and to the mountains. Then she understood, both being sacred symbols in the traditions of their fathers. Zeram stirred the coals.

"Where are the people who were here?"

Mara gave the sign of no knowledge. "I believe they fled from the king, since he once sought their leader's life, but it is something unknown to me."

"You came here to find them," he said slowly, his dark eyes studying her face. "Did you think they would still be here?"

"It was my hope."

"And so you fled the city, seeking those of your kind, and yet you say you do not seek to find your father and the other king's priests," he stated, the doubt in his voice obvious.

"These people were here before your warriors attacked us. Do you not see how long a time has passed since the altar was used? You seek Cumeni and the other priests. They are not the same as those who worshiped in this place."

Zeram pulled the two charred fish from the fire, tossing them onto a flat rock. "Then why have you left the safety of the Nephite city to seek them?"

Mara sighed and pulled her knees up, resting her arms there. "Is not freedom a greater thing than safety?"

Zeram thought this over, breaking the fish open which caused steam to rise up. "You seek these people so that you may live in freedom?"

"Yes," she answered at last. "And something more."

He picked up a piece of the meat, putting it in his mouth, then he signaled her to eat. "What more do you seek?"

Mara struggled with what she should say. "It is a difficult thing to tell of. They have something which I would have, or rather they have teachings which I desire to learn."

This surprised Zeram more than anything and he sat back, studying her. "What learning shall a woman be given?"

Mara didn't immediately answer. Instead she reached into her bundle and took out two neas, setting one on his side of the rock. Then she picked up some of the savory white meat, tasting it.

"There is a learning for all, bond and free, male and female," she stated at last, remembering what Riplah had once said. "It is a desirable thing, one which I thirsted after as my mentor taught me. Yet he is gone now these past two years, so I seek others who teach those same things."

"Teachings for all?"

"Yes, a truth for all to partake of."

"Bond and free, male and female," he said slowly, picking up the neas and breaking the skin. "Nephite and Lamanite?"

Mara laughed in amazement at such a statement. "How shall a Lamanite listen to the teachings of a Nephite?"

Zeram took a bite of the fruit. "Then it is not for all."

"Yes, it is for all. Yet does the puma come to the suckling lamb, that he might learn?"

He leaned across the fire, studying her. "What could the lamb offer?"

Mara's heart beat a little faster, uncertain at the course their conversation took. How could someone like Zeram understand? The traditions of their two people were so different that they shared little common ground. "If these teachings are not for you, it is only because you would choose not to have them," she softly answered.

Zeram's gaze didn't waver and the intensity of it brought heat to Mara's face.

"That is because they are worthless to me. Can the lamb teach the warrior how to fight, or how to overthrow his enemy?" he asked.

"You have no understanding of what these teachings are," she answered.

"I think they have no value. If it is not knowledge of how to fight and be the victor, it is of little use."

Mara stood, looking down at him in a thoughtful manner. "Do you think strength is only shown in fighting? I believe there is greater strength in learning the manner of peace."

He snorted in disgust and also stood. "So then peace is the teachings of the Nephites you seek?"

"It is part."

"My experience has taught me that your people talk well of peace, yet they use deceit and steal what is ours. How many times have we accepted peace from your kind only to have them use it against us? Your fathers wronged my fathers in the wilderness. They took the symbols of power, and used deceit to steal them away in the night. Even to this day the Nephites do the same thing, stealing what is not theirs."

Mara had steadily grown more pale, and she felt anger at his accusations. "I have taken nothing from you!"

"Your father and his men stole away my sister. What recompense will you make for that?"

"I can give you nothing."

"Then perhaps I will take repayment. Is not the law an eye for an eye? Or in this thing, a maid for a maid? If I cannot find my sister, then perhaps your father should repay what he has stolen with his own flesh."

Mara stared at him in stunned dismay. "You cannot lay your sister's abduction at my father's charge, nor expect repayment from me."

"You yourself said he was one of the king's priests who did this thing."

"Yet I do not even know if Cumeni still lives. And even if he does, to me he is dead. There are no bonds between us, so why should you expect me to repay a debt I did not make?"

Zeram sat down on the large stone, studying her. "I gave your people, and you, compassion. Twice now our soldiers have spared your lives, and once I stayed the sword from spilling your blood. Now your people, if not your father, have taken away that which was precious to me. How patient shall I be in waiting for justice?"

"You ask justice from me, because you gave mercy?" Mara asked.

He didn't answer, instead watched her walk away. She stood at the edge of the water, peering across the shimmering expanse, her posture tense. There was anger in her stance, her expression sober despite the fair features.

Zeram didn't know what it was about the Nephite maiden that intrigued him so. Certainly no other woman spoke as freely or with the skill of a man. Not a quality valued by his people, still he felt much interest in the things she said. Mara was very different from Saphira and the other women of his tribe, and yet he admired her. She spoke boldly and with courage, and parried his words in a manner he would not have abided from most women.

He studied the graceful line of her form and the way her tangled hair fell down her back, carved from the color of golden wood. Mara was a woman of worth, one whose value was evident. If he could not find Saphira he would always mourn the loss. But he would take recompense from those who had done this thing, by claiming this most prized Nephite possession.

CHAPTER EIGHT

The air was cool and silent as Zeram stalked the wild goat to have meat they could prepare and then travel with. As he stepped quietly through the dense brush, his lance was ready should he find the goat that continued to evade him. His plans hadn't changed, despite the despair he felt at being unable to find Saphira. Still, looking for her was his goal, even though the Nephite maiden had complicated things. He wouldn't leave Mara here, regardless of what she said. And though her words seemed true enough about why she had come here, still part of him wondered if she might know the places where her father would hide.

So intent was he on following the trail, he didn't see the wild boar until he had nearly run into it.

The boar bristled at being caught unaware, and bolted forward, its huge head bent low. At the charge of the boar, Zeram moved back and countered with his spear, which caught in the large tusks and snapped. Despite his swift leap to the side, the beast turned sharply and knocked him off balance, goring him just as he drew his short dagger. In his struggle with the beast, Zeram didn't immediately feel the pain of his wound. He concentrated solely on surviving this ordeal, and thrusting his dagger into the belly of the animal, he felt the boar shudder as it made a terrible squeal before drawing back.

Zeram stared into the small, hideous eyes, at the foaming snout and yellow tusks. As the animal charged again, Zeram summoned all his strength to meet the boar head on, so that when it caught him full force he drove the blade straight into the boar's chest cavity between its shoulderblade and neck. The boar grunted in pain and collapsed heavily upon the wounded Lamanite, who, gasping for breath, pulled himself from beneath the weight of the animal's head.

Freed from the weight of the boar, but not the pain of torn flesh, Zeram lay on his back, staring up at the piece of sky he could glimpse through the giant trees.

Blood oozed from his abdomen where the swine had gored and bitten him. Pain made his vision dim and he felt he might soon die. He wondered if Mara would come, yet why would the maiden look for him? When he didn't return to her camp by the waters she would certainly leave.

Zeram could feel darkness wash over him, the pain shoving him to that end, but he wouldn't allow it. Instead he rolled to his hands and knees, clinging to a tree to gain the strength to stand. His legs nearly collapsed beneath him yet he clung to a branch until the weakness passed. In the distance he could see the shimmering line that was water and he staggered in that direction.

How he made it to the shore, fighting waves of weakness and pain, he couldn't guess. Collapsing to his knees, then falling onto the sand, he succumbed to the darkness.

Mara put on a clean tunic and then plaited her wet hair. She had taken advantage of Zeram's absence to bathe and wash her soiled clothing. Returning to camp she sat down by the fire, waiting for the Lamanite to return. He had told her that he would be only a short distance away and that she must not flee. Yet now, in the silence of the clearing, Mara wondered if she could hastily gather her things and head across the northward ridge.

Certainly Zeram would continue the search for his sister and forget about herself. What would he care if she were to slip away? Perhaps he wouldn't be able to find her, thinking she had gone back to the city of Nephi. With these hopeful thoughts Mara quickly bundled her things together, hurrying along the edge of the water. Frequently glancing behind her she didn't immediately see the place ahead where the shore curved away, and in a moment she halted. A short distance from her there lay the form of a man, still as death, and when she drew closer she recognized Zeram.

Dropping her bundle she ran forward, kneeling down. He lay on his back, the flesh of his abdomen torn and bleeding, his face still. Placing her palm over his mouth, she felt for the slight brush of air that told her he lived. A few brief moments passed as Mara tried to think what to do. First she caught up her bundle and untied it, wadding the cloth and pressing it against the wounds to stop the flow of blood.

Sitting beside the large Lamanite, staring at his ashen face, a thought came to her. She could flee, safe in knowing he would never be able to follow. Yet immediately after the first thought came a second. She had a memory of this same man, his sword raised as she knelt and asked for mercy. His following actions had shown true compassion and she owed Zeram a debt for the kindness given. Now, she knew, the time had come to repay it.

Leaving him for a moment, Mara ran to a place where she had seen the healing plant growing in abundance. Hastily she gathered the stems and leaves, catching them in the hem of her tunic. Then she ran back to him, casting the plants down on her open shawl. Looking through the bundle she found the small gourd bowl she looked for and used it to bring water from the lake. Kneeling beside him, and carefully pulling back the cloth now soaked with blood, Mara grimaced at the awful sight and murmured, "What has happened to you, Zeram? Are these the marks of a lion or some other wild beast?" But unconscious, he made no reply.

She poured the water over his wounds then hurried back to the lake. Many times she filled the gourd, and many times returned to him to wash away the blood and foam. Then she used a small piece of cloth to repeatedly wipe dirt and blood out of the wounds. She did this many times, grateful that he seemed to have fainted from the pain as he stirred only a little. By the time she had finished cleansing his wounds, she was certain he had been attacked by a wild beast. Purple bruises were beginning to develop along his ribs and his breathing remained shallow. Using the gourd and a smooth stone from the lake, she made a paste of the plant stems. When this was ready she carefully packed the wounds with it.

"This is of the healing plant," she said, speaking to Zeram even though she knew he heard nothing. "It will kill any evil that remains from the beast."

Mara continued to talk to him, covering the wounds and salve with the leaves and binding it in place with torn strips of what had once been one of her head cloths. The second cloth she used to cover him, even though the air was warm. Then she sat beside him, shaken. Would he die? Once she wouldn't have cared, yet now Mara only hoped for his survival.

Looking at his face, free of expression, she saw fine, straight features, a strong brow, nose and mouth. Black hair fell back from his brow, his lips still in repose. He lay helpless beneath her ministrations, unaware even of her presence. Mara reached up, stroking his brow with her hand. Already the evil of the beast made his brow warm, yet she felt it a good omen, believing his body battled an evil spirit. At least he didn't bear the cold touch of the dead.

Leaving him for a moment she went to the waters, cleansing the blood from the cloth she had used and putting it on a boulder to dry. Knowing she couldn't move him back to the place where they had camped, instead Mara built a small pile of twigs nearby which she could light from the other fire. Then she hastened back to her earlier camp sight, gathering up his few things and carrying fire on a twig. She returned to where he lay, lighting the pile of twigs. Once the fire crackled and gave off its heat she felt safer, hoping that the beast which had attacked Zeram would not return.

How long she sat beside him, checking his wounds for bleeding, adding fuel to the fire to keep him warm, stroking his brow and murmuring words of comfort, Mara didn't know. Yet sitting beside him, tending him as if he were the most helpless infant, a quiet calm overcame her. Her foe no longer seemed so fierce, nor did he fit the image within her fearful dreams. This man, though not of her people, was as any other man, fallible and vulnerable.

The day grew old and evening settled across the waters, darkening the depths. Mara put more wood on the fire and then gathered enough to keep it burning through the night. When she got back she skinned the small animal Zeram had caught earlier, cooking the meat. Her attention focused on removing the meat from the fire, she didn't see Zeram awake, yet when he moaned she quickly turned to him.

"Zeram?"

He looked at her, his eyes glazed with pain. "I killed the wild swine," he said, his voice a mere rasp.

Mara's eyes widened. "Is that the animal which attacked you?" Wonderment filled her voice, for certainly there was no more deadly beast than the boar. She placed her cool hand on his brow. "You must eat, and then rest."

She moved to the fire and the meat, using a narrow blade to peel off strips. These she brought to Zeram, placing small pieces in his mouth. He chewed the food with effort, knowing that he needed strength.

At last he asked in a somewhat stronger voice, "Why have you done this thing?"

Mara knew what he meant. It was evident to him that she had every opportunity now to leave him. "I thought of leaving," she confessed. "But I also remembered the time that you spared my life."

Zeram thoughtfully chewed the meat and drank the bitter brew she had made from the healing leaves. Then he laid back, closing his eyes. "Will you leave now?"

Mara pondered his words, and the quiet voice that had spoken them. "No, I will not."

Nothing more was said between them. Mara added more twigs to the fire, fearful other wild beasts might come in the darkness. Then she laid down near Zeram, hopeful he would survive the night.

For many days Mara tended him, cleaning his wounds and making him hot drinks of the healing plant and the flower of a herb she found for easing pain. Zeram slept for most of the time, and Mara busied herself with weaving fibers from the rope plant, making a net. She then laid along a ledge that hung over the waters and with the net in the water patiently waited for fish she could snatch up. At first it took her such a long time she nearly despaired, until she finally caught a large fish, jerking the net out of the water and throwing it on the shore. Zeram was awake when she brought the fish back to camp, and his look of surprised admiration filled Mara with pride.

The days passed and Mara added to their stores with wild

neas and berries, and roots of the sweet plant that she dug up. When they tired of fish she managed to snare two wild doves, returning to camp with them. She plucked and cleaned them, wrapping the meat in leaves and roasting it in hot coals. Zeram leaned up on one elbow, watching her.

"You have provided well for us," he stated.

Mara turned from the fire, smiling at him for the praise given. She gathered up her healing supplies and knelt beside him. "It is time I check your wounds."

Zeram obediently lay down on his back, his arms beneath his head. In the past few days he had begun to feel much better, sitting up to eat and even moving about the camp. He stared up at Mara, who busied herself with removing the leaves. Then she washed the wounds with water, pleased how they had healed. The cuts were still red, their lines jaggedly meshed together, but in time they would fade although he would always carry the scars. She touched the lines of the wound.

"Is there pain?"

Zeram studied her, his eyes fastened on the face he had come to know so well. He often gained pleasure from looking on the soft curve of her mouth, the finely arched brows over light brown eyes, the line of her jaw. At the moment her hair fell unbound except for a narrow purple headcloth across her brow. She knelt close enough to him that he could have reached up and caught a strand of her hair.

"There is no pain, Mara," he stated, yet his voice drew her gaze to his.

"Something troubles you," she said, and he looked away, disconcerted by the way she could peer into the depths of him.

During the days of his illness he had come to depend on her for his very survival. Each time he awoke he expected to find her gone, yet each time she was there, ministering to his wounds and continuing to care for him. He felt a heaviness in his heart that he didn't understand.

Mara touched his wounds again and he grew tense. She immediately put her hand on his brow, fearful the fever had returned. Zeram reached up, taking her hand in his. Then he pushed himself into a sitting position, facing her.

"Mara, my wounds have healed well enough. Soon we can travel."

She lowered her eyes, but not before he saw the alarm in them. "I have not thought of traveling these past days," she said.

"You could have left. A more cunning maiden would not have hesitated to leave her enemy here."

"I do not think of you as my enemy," she answered in a low voice, yet pulled her hand from his.

Zeram reached out, touching her face with his fingers and raised her gaze to his own. "You have done well by me. I would have died without your kindness."

A slight smile touched Mara's lips. "I have only sought to repay the debt of your mercy, for the compassion given to myself and my people. Tell me now, Zeram of the Lamanites, is the debt paid in full?"

Zeram grew thoughtful, his dark eyes assessing her. "Yes, it is so," he answered at last, and then his voice softened. "The truth would have me say the debt is paid." They were both quiet and then he smiled. "You are a woman of exception, Mara. Your kindness, the toil and patience you have shown in caring for me, are much admired."

"You talked of traveling," she said, her voice low. "When we leave this place, things between us will change. If I go back to the city of Nephi I will once again be the captive of your people."

"We could stay here," he said. "This is an abundant land with its waters and forests."

"What of your sister?"

The question twisted his heart and for the first time he looked away, pain in his eyes. "So much time has passed. I must face the truth. Saphira is lost to me."

"Will you return to your people alone, then?"

Zeram spread his hands on his knees, thoughts struggling within him. "If I return to my own city, will you come with me?"

The words once spoken made silence a barrier between them. At last Mara sighed. "I would be hated among your people. They would only see me as a daughter of their foe."

Zeram knew her words were true, yet his mind could see no way. "I cannot abandon you."

Mara smiled. "I have taken care of myself these past days, and tended you, wounded and helpless."

A brief scowl touched his brow, but when she laughed it eased. "It is so," he admitted. Then he grew sober again. "Where will you go, Mara?"

She glanced away, stopping her gaze before it reached the ridge. Zeram didn't need her to look to the place she would go. He knew. Many times he had seen her wistful stare, the look that told of traveling far and of fretful worry that she tarried too long in tending him.

"You have seen me gather the leaves of the healing plant," she said at last. "I grind them into a balm that must be put on your wounds every day. There is a large crop of it beyond that boulder. You must gather them before you travel." She sounded almost unhappy.

"I will not let you go, Mara," he said, reaching out and catching a stray lock of her hair, then tucking it gently into the band of cloth she wore.

"You have no claim on me, now that the debt has been paid," she replied, a hard edge to her words.

Zeram didn't answer, his expression revealing the discomfort he had felt earlier. He stood and walked to the edge of the waters, his posture betraying the defeat he felt.

The glass surface of the lake reflected the dark blue of the sky, cloud shadows changing the face of the waters. Zeram felt the mood of the lake, felt its changes mirrored within him. Turmoil strained his breathing and he despised the weakness that still plagued his body. He felt weak in spirit as well, almost fearful of the tenderness he felt for the Nephite maiden.

Zeram couldn't understand the emotions that fought within him, striking out against all that he had been raised to believe. Everything that had once been truth seemed a falsehood. Were not the people of the maiden his enemy? How many times had they deceived him, even his fathers, from the beginning? He and his kin had shown mercy in not destroying them from off the face of the land, even though at one time it had been his greatest wish. Yet somehow being with the maiden had changed him, for how could he destroy her people having once known her?

He sat down on a boulder by the water, reminding himself that it was Mara's very kinsman who had stolen his sister. Even now thoughts of what evils had befallen Saphira gnawed at him, filling him with the old fear and anger that had made him travel into the wilderness searching for her in the first place.

From the side of his gaze he could see Mara preparing the fowl she had taken from the fire, seasoning it with herbs dried on a rock by the flames. He watched her place the meat on a flat piece of bark, bringing it to him. Silently she handed him the food, then returned to the fire.

Zeram ate the meat in its seasoned juices, still staring across the water, watching the setting sun lay its long golden tresses across the expanse. Then he looked at the mountains, and the ridge that went between them. He had seen Mara study the pass when she thought he slept. Did she seek her father, despite her claims that he was dead to her, or did she truly seek the people who would teach her? Another thought came to him. Perhaps the priests who had stolen Saphira and the others also knew of the people she sought. If so Mara could lead him to them.

Suddenly his heart felt less burdened, the decision having been made. He would not return to his people, his desires were not there. Neither would he wander through the forests trying to find those who had taken his sister. There was another way. Zeram stood, walking over to the fire and sitting beside it. He peered through the waft of smoke at Mara.

"I have made my decision. Tomorrow we travel back to my people."

He saw the alarm in her eyes, yet kept his own expression sober. He didn't want to lie to Mara, but knew that such a statement would force her to try to make the attempt to flee during the night. He couldn't risk having her leave when he wasn't watching. This way he would be able to follow her.

"You are not well enough to travel," she stammered.

"I have gained much strength these last two days."

"Can we not stay here a while longer?"

Zeram lifted his hand to quell her argument. "Tomorrow."

Mara watched the golden colors of the sun die upon the clouds and the mountain ridges, the sky fading into shades of darkness. At that hushed moment of eventide, when all the land seemed calm, Mara felt tense with fear. She had been pushed to the decision she knew was coming.

For many days now she had delayed her plans in order to care for the Lamanite, and during that time had come to see that he was not the fearful warrior of her dream, but a man of flesh like all others. Through the days of his pain he had been longsuffering, never ordering her about or demanding attention as another might have. He often spoke to her with a gentleness she hadn't seen for a long time, even among her own kinsmen. Yet his people and their ways were strange to her and she knew she could not return with him.

When the sky darkened and the stars flickered like far distant fires, Mara laid down on her bed of leaves, covering herself with a shawl. The words he had spoken echoed through her mind, willing her to stay awake. Tonight she must flee.

CHAPTER NINE

*Z*eram leaned against the jagged rock, trying to breathe more easily. He wondered at the foolishness of his plan. He hadn't realized how weak the attack of the boar had left him, nor how fleet the maiden would be. His plan to follow Mara had seemed simple, yet putting it into effect proved more difficult than he had supposed. He had lost sight of her some time before, although he still followed her trail.

The mountain ridge was steep, the air cool and thin. Zeram looked back across the view where the waters lay in shimmering splendor at the feet of the mountains, forests edging the banks. He turned again to his task, forcing himself to go on, fearful that with every break in his stride Mara further eluded him. He followed the narrow ledge around the mountain cliff, guarding his steps, until the ridge widened onto a small mesa.

Here Zeram immediately halted, for he found Mara sitting on an outcropping of boulders, her eyes on him, with a look that told him she had been waiting for him. He felt a moment of humiliation before he walked towards her.

Mara stood, her eyes glancing over him and resting on his face. "How have you made it this far?" Her voice was not gentle.

"Your place is not to question me, woman," he stated.

Mara looked at him only a moment before standing and catching up her things. She moved to leave.

"Wait," he commanded, his body willing him to sit and rest where his pride demanded that he stand. As he watched her turn back, he saw in her stance something close to condescending patience, which made him speak more harshly than he might have otherwise. Pointing to the water bag she carried, he said brusquely, "Fetch me water."

Mara lifted the bag to her hip, unbound the water plug, and poured water into the small gourd that attached to it. Then she brought it to Zeram, who had carefully sat his aching body on a large boulder. He took the gourd, his eyes never leaving her face while he drank. Then he handed the cup back, his fingers brushing hers.

"You knew I followed," he said stiffly.

Mara closed the bag and slid the handle of the gourd over the top. "I heard you on the mountain. I waited to see if you would make it this far, or fall from the cliff."

He scowled and she shrugged, sitting down on a rock opposite him. "You have chosen to follow me. Last night you threatened me that we would return to the land of your fathers, so that I would flee. I did not see it at first, but watching you struggle up the mountain the understanding came. Why do you follow me, Zeram?"

"I owe no answer to a woman. You forget your place."

Mara felt her face grow warm with anger, even though how he spoke was the way of their people. "It is true, but here there are no laws, and you are not the stronger now. You are still weak, Zeram, and I will say what I will, you cannot stop me. I can flee now, and how shall you catch me? These past days I have tended your wounds and cared for you enough to know how much strength you have gained. I chose to come back here. And if I had not, you would not have found me."

His eyes were on her. "Why did you come back, then?"

She took in a long, slow breath, her expression thoughtful. "The days I cared for you took much toil to preserve your life. I would not have you toss it away out of carelessness. But neither will I stay if your intent is to bring me back to your homeland."

Zeram's posture eased. He looked across the jagged mountains. "Where are you going, Mara?"

The quiet of his voice startled her. "I go to seek Alma and his followers," she answered.

"How do you know where they are?"

When she didn't answer he looked back at her. Mara's hand touched the place where the gold glyph lay next to her skin. "I have been shown the way in a sign."

He looked puzzled. "What do you mean, a sign?"

"Alma left it for the followers of Christ," she said at last, as if sharing with him something gravely important to her. "Those who believe on him would know the sign and would travel northward from the waters. This place alone crosses northward over the mountains. Somewhere, beyond there, are the people I seek."

Zeram somehow knew she spoke the truth. "Who is Christ?" he asked.

Mara looked back at him, feeling the cool of the mountain air, the stillness of the moment. Her earlier concerns faded and she sat beside him. "Christ is the Anointed One. He is the Lord our God who will come to earth someday. He is also the Son of God, and does the will of the Father."

Zeram was thoughtful. He remembered an old story from his childhood about the Great Spirit, but could not recall much about it. "Who is this Alma, then, and what does he have to do with your God?"

"He teaches of Christ. He and his people fled from our king because they believed in the Anointed One, and King Noah forbade them."*

"If you believe on this Christ, why did you not join them? Why do you wait until now?"

"Because I was only taught by Riplah, my mother's father, who wanted me to find them."

* Mosiah 18:1-3

She paused at the expression on Zeram's face who asked soberly, "The old man you mourned for after the battle?"

"Yes. He was a true follower of Christ, and taught me while we lived in the house of my father. Riplah would have joined with Alma, except he would not forsake me." She paused, thinking of the father who had forsaken her for his own life, while Riplah had sacrificed all not to forsake her.

She bent her head, sudden misery in her movement. "I promised Riplah even as he died that I would seek what he spoke of as the living water, that is, the Christ. I only know the few things Riplah taught me, and had only begun to learn when he died. He sacrificed much to stay and teach me. If I do not find Alma and the others, then I betray him."

Zeram pondered all she spoke, the intensity of her words binding themselves on his heart. "Then perhaps it is time you kept the promise you made. I will help you find these followers of Christ."

Mara lifted widened eyes to him. "You will help me?"

"Yes."

"For what purpose?"

He didn't immediately answer, yet when he did his voice seemed in great contrast to the first words of their encounter. "I would have perished if you had not cared for me."

"That is true, Zeram," she answered. "And yet I would have perished had you not stopped the war. You owe me no debt in this thing."

Zeram felt a softening within that was strange to him. "Perhaps," he said at last, "If I help you find these people I will also find your father and the others. There is no other place to seek, unless I choose to abandon my undertaking and return to my people."

Mara thought this over, and although she didn't believe Cumeni and the priests would ever join those they once sought to kill, she did not disagree with him. Instead her heart filled with happiness, because for the first time she was not alone in her search. She moved forward, kneeling by Zeram and resting her arms on the boulder where he sat. She smiled at him.

"I am most grateful, Zeram."

He looked into her face, at the dark golden hair falling back from her fair brow, and at the tender eyes meeting his. "I well remember that day you knelt before me," he said quietly. "I shall not soon forget your plea for mercy. I did not hear the others, only one."

Mara lowered her gaze. "It was a terrible day, and one I will never forget."

She stood and Zeram looked up at her. "Is mercy such a terrible gift?" he finally asked.

"Mercy from one who once was my enemy, and none from my own father?" she answered.

He was thoughtful. Then he reached out, catching the end of the sash that tied her brown tunic. "What does this Alma teach about mercy?"

A soft smile touched her mouth, replacing the more sober line once there. "I do not know. If we find him, I shall ask."

Zeram thought this over, then stood. He need say nothing more. Mara caught up her things and followed behind him towards the second mountain.

They traveled along the ridge in silence, crossing between the high hills. The scent of cool mountain air and the warmth of sunlight on their backs made the journey pleasant. Their progress was slow, Mara walking behind Zeram in the manner of their people. She now felt much happiness that she had chosen to turn back and meet him on the mountain. When she had first realized he followed her she had been angry and fearful, but now the plan began to fall into place. The God of whom Riplah had once taught her had now provided a way, for certainly with Zeram's aid she would find the people of Alma.

Later in the day they passed through a wide place between the mountain ridges where many people and their flocks had camped, though much time had passed. This filled Mara with hope, proving to her that Alma and his followers had taken this direction. Beyond the narrow valley she stopped two different times, not because she felt weary but because she knew Zeram needed to rest. The second time she delayed him with talk, knowing that he would not admit his need to rest.

"Zeram, tell me of your sister," she asked.

He remained silent for a moment, his dark eyes peering into the distance. "I grew up watching over Saphira. Even though she was only a girl child my parents felt great fondness for her."

"And fondness for yourself, also?"

"Yes, since I was the son of their old age, and she their daughter. My mother was barren many years, and yet my father would not take another wife. She bore much scourge among the women, then she conceived in her old age and bare a son and a daughter of the same womb."

"Ah," Mara said, obviously impressed. "Such a thing is most rare." She leaned forward, studying Zeram in a new light. Her eyes glanced over his well muscled form and the black hair that fell like a dark mane about his handsome face.

"You must have been a child of great pride to her," she said in a thoughtful voice. "What did the others who had ridiculed her say?"

"Our mother's name became revered among the people, and she was given great honor to replace the shame of her years."

His story touched Mara and she smiled. "Your mother was a great woman, then, to be blessed in this manner. And your father, he was a leader?"

"Yes, and a strong warrior."

"It is a good thing you have, knowing the strength of your father and mother."

"What of your kinsmen?" he asked. "Are there any in the city you left behind?"

Mara leaned back against the cliff of dark rock, her hair like a shaft of sunlight against the stone. "I have no noble heritage to tell, not as yours. Yet I remember my mother when I was a child, before she died. Her eyes were kind, her voice soft and always giving comfort. I remember thinking she was beautiful, and knowing my father loved her very much. He had no other, then. But when she died he turned from the teachings of his fathers and followed after the king. Cumeni took many concubines. I believe some of them gave him children, but they never came to our dwelling." She looked away, the shame she felt obvious. Then she continued.

"When Riplah was dying I told him that Cumeni had deserted us. He said something I now see as the truth, that my father had deserted me long before that day on the hill. I never saw it so clearly until this moment, though."

"Is not the heritage of the man Riplah a noble thing? You speak often of his wisdom."

Mara pushed back some strands of hair that had fallen across her cheek, her fingers caught in the tresses she pulled back. "Yes," she said, her voice thoughtful. "It was he who sent us down the hill that day to plead before the Lamanite warriors."

Zeram leaned near, looking into the face whose symmetry and softness pleased him. Each day he came to know this face in greater detail, to see the mouth that expressed the feelings of a woman and held him fascinated. To see a gentle brow and eyes the color of afternoon light. Those same eyes met his own.

"He was wise, indeed," Zeram said, letting out a slow breath. "To send the fairest of all the Nephite maidens to charm her foe, and win the compassion of their captain."

A flush of color heightened Mara's cheeks, and Zeram stood as they again took up their journey northward.

That night they camped beneath a grove of mountain cedars, then traveled on at first light. By noon the next day they stopped beside a small mountain spring, the beginning source of a stream that fell from the face of the cliff into a pool far below. A source of water was considered a sacred token among their people, a symbol of life. Near the spring an altar had been built from stones, and in her heart Mara knew that those she sought had offered sacrifice in this place. Farther down the mountain was a vein of obsidian, which Zeram noted had been partially mined by the others who had come before.

"There are good omens found on this journey," he said.

Mara smiled up at him, "Yes, it is so."

Zeram did not say what he really felt, that they were in need of many good omens because the expanse which lay before them filled him with trepidation. The mountain sloped down into a narrow valley, through which ran three small rivers. Yet beyond that lay a massive, tangled jungle. And though he peered to the horizon of distant hills, there was no sign of any other people. Perhaps he had been foolish to follow Mara in what she sought, instead of forcing her to return with him to his people.

"Before we enter the forests I will need to make new weapons," he said, kneeling down at the outcropping of black glass and examining pieces, carefully selecting those he would use.

"And I will fill our water bag from the spring," she said, turning back behind the jagged rocks.

Zeram pulled a narrow splitting stone from the pouch he carried, setting the pieces of obsidian before him on a flat rock. He sat down with the tool and carefully split a narrow piece of obsidian from the larger black rock. Holding the long narrow piece in a folded strip of leather with one hand he started to meticulously chip moon shaped slivers off of the edges by pressing firmly down with a pointed horn chipper. Patiently he worked the obsidian to a slicing point, then turned it over. He continued to work the other edge until it became very sharp, making a large spear head. Down in the forest he would find a straight branch and fashion a lance to replace the one that broke during the boar's attack.

Next Zeram took a long, narrow piece of the glassy rock, carefully slicing away the sides to make a sharp knife. It was not as long as the sword he had left at home, still it would serve its purpose without being cumbersome. He used the knife to cut a strip of leather from the goat hide he carried, binding it tightly about the handle so that the obsidian wouldn't cut him. Testing it for weight and comfort, he was satisfied. Then he wrapped the spear head in the skin along with a number of smaller pieces that would make good arrow points. These he put inside a goat-stomach pouch to use when he could make a bow once they reached the forest.

Standing, he slipped the knife handle into the girdle of his breech cloth. He thought of Mara, who had not come to talk to him during any of the time that he worked, and he turned back up the narrow way that led to the spring. After climbing up the side of the rill he spied her and stopped, wondering at what he saw.

Not far from the spring Mara knelt on the ground, her head bent down, her hands clasped together. A strange feeling came over Zeram and he peered closely, seeing that her lips moved as she quietly spoke. While he stood watching her, she ceased talking, opened her eyes, and lifted her head. When she glanced up her gaze fell on Zeram, and he suddenly felt awkward, knowing he had intruded on something he didn't understand. Mara smiled shyly, arose and walked over to him. She questioned him with her eyes.

Drawing the obsidian blade from his girdle, he assumed an awkward formality. "I have made a spear head and this knife."

"It is fine workmanship," she replied, studying the sharp edge.

He put the knife back, suddenly asking the thing he had not planned to speak of. "Mara, what was that you were doing?"

Surprised, she answered, "I was praying."

"What is praying?"

Mara was still more surprised at this unexpected question. Even before learning how to pray from Riplah, she had seen the priest at the temple as they prayed, and grieving women at the outer wall. "When I pray," she answered slowly, trying to think of the words to explain, "I talk to God."

"That is most peculiar," he mused aloud.

"Zeram, how shall he give us aid if I do not ask?"

The Lamanite grew thoughtful. "Is this the same one, the Christ, that you pray to?"

"No, Instead I pray to the Father, in the name of Jesus Christ. This is the way that Riplah taught. Did your mother never pray?"

"My people do not believe as yours."

"Many of my own people no longer believe, either. But

Riplah once told me that this was the way of our ancient father Lehi, and his family, when they traveled to this land."

Zeram didn't want to talk of that, for it reminded him of the old hatred he had lived with all his life. Yet looking down at the Nephite maiden he felt there must have been some good among her ancestors. They walked back to the out-cropping of volcanic glass. "When you talk to God, does he speak?"

Mara struggled with an answer. "I think he may speak," she said at last. "But I do not yet know how to listen well enough. I have prayed before and he has answered, but he has not spoken."

She stopped, looking out over the expanse of jungle. "This is a difficult thing to tell, Zeram. Twice I have had an answer. The first was at the altar down by the Waters of Mormon. From my prayer I discovered the sign that told me to travel north."

"What of the second?"

"It was back there, the prayer I only just spoke."

"Why did you pray?"

"Because when I looked across this," she said, pointing to the scene below the mountain. "I felt fearful, wondering how we shall find the others. Yet when I knelt beside the sacred spring, near the place where sacrifice had been of-fered, a great calm came over my spirit."

Mara looked up into the face of the man she was coming to know, standing beside him on the mountain. She placed her hand on his arm. "All will be well, Zeram. I feel we shall find that which we seek."

Zeram didn't know what to say, pondering on the words Mara had spoken with such quiet assurance. Then he took her hand in his, holding it warm within his grasp. He led her down the mountain.

CHAPTER TEN

*Z*eram glanced back at the shrouded jungle he had just passed through, taking note of a malformed tree that would help mark his way back to camp. During their travels, and the times he needed to go hunt for food, he had learned to keep an everchanging map in his mind that would always lead him back to Mara.

He followed an animal trail that wound upward, eventually finding himself atop a ridge. The land dropped away and as Zeram scanned the expanse his eyes caught something that made him halt. Below, in a small clearing, he saw a woman. Zeram felt his throat constrict, his heart hammering wildly. She was far away, her tunic only a smudge of crimson beneath black locks, yet even at this distance he knew her. He scanned the surrounding area and then froze. Not far from the clearing was a man laying a snare. A Nephite!

Zeram raced down the ridge, heedless of the branches that slapped at him, all the while his mind sending out a warning. Where were the other Nephites? How did Saphira come to be alone with this single enemy? Zeram formed a quick plan. He must kill the Nephite and escape with his sister before the others returned.

Samuel lay on his belly, peering through the ferns at the snare he had laid. He held his breath watching the fat bird land near the hemp, not daring to make any sound that would cause it to fly away. His fingers held the vine, eager to jerk it closed, and yet he forced himself to wait.

The bird flapped its wings, stepped away and then stepped near, pecking at the seeds set in a small pile on the ground. Once it began eating it grew less cautious, and Samuel suddenly pulled the rope tight in a quick movement, snaring the fowl's talon. It let out a wild screech, flying upwards, but he jerked the rope down, bringing the bird to earth in a flurry of feathers. He quickly snapped its neck, then coiled the vine, the bird hanging from the end.

Pleased with his catch, he headed back in the direction where Saphira was working to start a fire. Samuel felt proud that they had seldom gone hungry and that he continued to provide meat and fish for their needs.

He had lost count of the days they traveled in the wilderness, trying to find their homeland. Because it had been years since he lived in the land of first inheritance he was not able to clearly remember the way back. And Saphira, never having been out of the Valley of Shemlon before, could not find the way, either. Still, they were not too distraught at being lost, and they had come to learn much about each other during their travel. Samuel admitted to himself that he didn't want to face the day when they finally found her people and he would be forced to leave her and flee for his life. Yet he also knew that they couldn't wander on through the forests indefinitely, and that Saphira was beginning to grow discouraged.

Not far from the small glade where they had spent the night, Samuel was deep in thought when a sudden movement caught his eye. He turned, his hand going to the hilt of his knife. At the same moment a man moved in before him. Samuel stepped back, dropping the bird and drawing his knife. A quick glance let him see the strong Lamanite features, a large frame, and a knife drawn and pointed at him. His enemy was formidable and he gripped his own blade, every muscle tense as the man cried out in rage and leapt at him.

Samuel twisted sideways as the Lamanite's knife cut close to him, his own blade hitting the leather band across the man's chest. Samuel's knife point broke under the pressure and the blade flipped away. He found himself pinned with his back to a giant sapota, his throat being squeezed in the man's fist. He could hear his racing heart pounding like a drum in his ears, cutting off the sound of wind-brushed leaves and the call of birds. He knew in another moment the warrior's blade would pierce his heart.

Zeram squeezed his fist tighter as the Nephite struggled for air, his knife pressed against the man's chest, ready to kill him. Every instinct told Zeram to destroy this Nephite, yet he did not. Instead the black blade of his knife stayed in a frozen dance against the man's chest until a sudden cry pierced the air.

A maiden ran towards them and his heart leapt. Saphira! She ran to him, her hands pulling at his arm. "Zeram," she desperately cried, trying to pull him away from the Nephite. "Do not harm him!"

Zeram stared down at Saphira, amazed at seeing her there, and even more amazed by her actions. "Let him go!" she wailed.

He ignored her plea, feeling renewed anger that she would plead for the life of this pitiful Nephite. Saphira pulled harder at his arm, desperately trying to jerk the knife away. "Stop!" she cried. "Zeram, I beg you to stop!"

Her tearful expression and fearful plea made him feel helpless and confused. How was he to rescue her if she did not allow him to kill her abductor?

"He is not our enemy, " she sobbed, her fingers grasping at his own where they squeezed Samuel's throat. Her effort was useless, no more capable than if she were a small bird clawing at him. Tears spilled down her cheeks. Finally she looked up into Zeram's eyes and her shuddering voice softened. "Please, dear brother, for my sake release him."

Zeram was more helpless against her tears than a sword. Slowly he lowered his knife and released his hold on the Nephite who crumpled to the ground, gasping for air. Zeram quickly scanned his sister, noting the soiled, ragged tunic she wore and her tear-streaked countenance.

"Saphira," he whispered, and then she flew into his arms. He embraced her, a fierce joy clenching his heart. "We must leave here at once before the other Nephites return," he said urgently.

"Be calm, my brother. There is no one here save us two, and we have traveled alone for many days."

Zeram relaxed his grip on Saphira and struggled to think things through, his chest still heaving from the heat of his struggle with the hated Nephite.

Samuel waited for the dizziness to pass, gulping in breaths of air. Finally he managed to rise to his feet, warily looking at the scene before him. Many thoughts raced through his mind: fear of losing Saphira, fear for himself now that he had unwittingly stumbled onto her people, anger at Zeram's attack and his own foolish lack of caution.

Zeram turned to stare at the man in front of him, quickly assessing his attire of animal skins and leggings. The man appeared near in age to himself, and though not as heavily muscled, stood nearly as tall. Despite his coarse attire he was obviously a Nephite.

Instinctively Zeram still felt the desire to strike, to cut him down before this foe sounded the alarm. But until he learned more from his sister he would do nothing. In a moment Saphira pulled from his arms, turning a smiling, tearful face to Samuel. "This is Zeram, my brother."

Samuel stared at the huge warrior and Saphira felt Zeram's arm grow tense beneath her fingers. She looked up at him and saw his angry eyes on Samuel. "Is this one of the Nephites who stole you away?" he asked in a dark voice.

Saphira turned to face her brother again, determination in her look. "He was one, but you will not harm him."

Zeram didn't acknowledge Saphira's demand, instead he faced the Nephite, his jaw clenched. "I swore a vow to kill those who took you," he said.

"And will you also kill the man who has fled from his own kind to return me to our people?" she asked.

Zeram's eyes flicked back to his sister. "This is true, my brother!" she insisted. "Put down your knife, and I will tell you all if you vow him no harm." When Zeram didn't move she sighed in exasperation. "Can you not cast aside your hatred of the Nephites for even a moment?"

Silence stood thick between the three, until at last Zeram lowered his knife. Saphira smiled, "I told Samuel we would find our way home."

Zeram took in a slow breath. "We are very far from home, my sister. I have traveled alone these many days to find you."

Tears again shimmered in Saphira's eyes. "I also told Samuel that you would come," she whispered.

For the first time she noticed the scars on his abdomen, concern filling her. "What has happened? Were you in a battle?"

"Only with a boar," Zeram said ruefully, then for the first time he smiled at seeing Saphira's look of awe. "I, too, have much to tell."

He walked over to the Nephite, openly assessing him. "Is what she has said, true?"

Samuel studied his opponent, recalling the things Saphira had said about her brother and knowing he faced a fierce Lamanite warrior. Yet even with what she had told him, he

hadn't been able to imagine how large of stature her kinsman would be when she herself was so delicate. The only
thing that gave him hope was learning that Zeram came alone,
and also that they hadn't traveled back into Shemlon.

Samuel spoke, his voice now hoarse from the tight grip
Zeram had held on his throat. "It is true that I promised
Saphira I would take her home. But it is also true that I was
with the men who stole the maidens."

"Samuel, you would have stayed their actions, but they
would not heed you," Saphira softly reminded.

"Still, I stole you from your people," he stated, boldly
facing the Lamanite who had every right to cut him down.

Saphira sighed and turned to Zeram. "The men who attacked planned to carry us all away, and another pursued me
into the river. Yet Samuel fought him for my sake, and because of his mercy I am unharmed."

Zeram felt a quiet amazement at her explanation. The
knowledge that her captor would most certainly have as-
saulted her had hung heavy on his heart. Now, to find her
here, safe beyond all his worst fears, filled him with tender
emotion. He didn't want to reveal his feelings, so he busied
himself with sheathing his knife, noting that the Nephite
still eyed him warily. His heart continued to race with the
thrill of the fight, and from the anger so recently felt. It seemed
awkward to be standing here with a man he had wanted to
slay only a few moments ago, but whom he now must acknowledge.

Despite the uncertainty in the other man's face, Zeram
extended his hand. "I owe you a great debt, Nephite."

Samuel didn't know what to think of this man who had
almost killed him, but he smiled in embarrassment as they
clasped forearms. "I have done a poor job of returning her home.
We have been wandering in the wilderness for many days, now."

Saphira leaned into her brother and he put his arm about her. Zeram then released Samuel's grasp and the three of them stood together. Zeram looked at Samuel. "When we found our women were stolen we took up arms and attacked the city of Nephi. Yet after the battle, when our king was fallen captive to your soldiers, the Nephites pleaded their innocence before us. They told of the priests of your King Noah, and laid the blame on them. I would know the truth."

Samuel pondered all he heard, especially learning for the first time that the city hadn't fallen. Amulon had lied, their people were not destroyed! "It is true," he said. "My father was one of the priests of the king, and it was the scheme of their leader, Amulon, to steal away the Lamanite daughters that they might have wives. And this because they would not face the shame of deserting their families by returning to the city."*

"I swore a vow to find the maidens and slay their captors," Zeram said.

"It has been many days since we left them," Saphira told him. "And even if we could find our way to them, the other maidens have chosen to stay with the men who took them. They would not escape with me when I fled."

Zeram thought over all he had heard. "I had nearly given up hope of ever finding you," he said, his voice thick with emotion.

Saphira laughed, brushing at her tears. "My joy, too, is great."

"Will you come to where we camp?" Samuel asked.

"I must go find Mara, and tell her that I have at last found my sister."

"Who is Mara?" Saphira asked, her eyes full of sudden curiosity. "You said you traveled alone."

"I meant that I came without warriors. Yet along the way I met another." He grew thoughtful, remembering Mara

* Mosiah 20:3

praying, and afterwards her saying that she knew they would find what they sought. He would ponder this thing later, he thought, and for now keep it in his heart. He motioned Saphira and Samuel to follow.

"I have left her alone too long, now. Come with me and I will tell what has happened."

Saphira and Samuel glanced at each other, and Saphira spoke. "Let me gather our few things from the clearing and we will come with you."

She hurried back through the trees while Samuel picked up the fowl and rewound the rope. In the quiet of the forest he said nothing, wondering at this strange turn and how it would affect his life. Zeram was also thoughtful, almost unbelieving that he had found his sister unharmed and well. In a moment Saphira returned and they walked with Zeram into the jungle. She asked him many things and marveled at the tale he told.

Mara tended the fire, adding twigs to the flames and watching them burn in colors of heat. When it grew hot enough she would skin and cook the small animal that Zeram had snared, but for now she sat, unplaiting her hair. It had been several days since they had left the Waters of Mormon and she longed for a place where she could bathe. But the jungle rivers were torrid and dangerous, with no shallow places to wash. So she satisfied herself with crushing leaves from the fragrant plant and running them through her hair. She took a comb from her bundle, working it through the tangles until her tresses fell in a smooth veil.

With the passing days of their journey Mara was beginning to lose the calm assurance she had felt on the mountain top. Descending into the valley they had been faced with a wild and strange land. It was difficult to travel through the thick underbrush and the rivers almost impossible to cross. It was also often warm in the forest, a contrast to the cool mountain region. Several times it had rained, turning suddenly wet and cold, but with the passing storm the air became even more thick and uncomfortable. They had passed through swarms of biting insects, forced to rub bitter leaves on their skin to repel them.

Mara tried to think again on her prayer on the mountain top, and the answer of calm she received. She clung to that intangible memory, reminding herself of what she had felt. Certainly somewhere out there were those she sought, and she forced her mind from discouragement. Her heart was always grateful that despite the difficulties of the journey Zeram was with her. It would have been impossible for her to travel alone, and her cause would have been hopeless.

Her heart softened when she thought of Zeram. How patiently he helped her, always willing to go on even though he was still somewhat weak from the attack. He didn't complain, or tell her that this scheme to find the others was impossible even when she herself grew discouraged. She daily marveled that he would travel with her through the wilderness, watching over her and giving aid in the search.

In the distant past there had been times when Zeram had frightened her, especially those when she had seen him in battle, a warrior against her kindred. But each day since their journey began she now saw a noble endurance in him that she had not found in any other of the Nephites, save her grandfather. And never before had any man deferred to her choice, nor set credence by what she said.

Mara admitted to herself that she had learned many things since leaving the city of Nephi. She discovered courage

in herself, and received understanding from the man whose
kinsmen were her people's enemy. Since childhood Mara had
been raised to hate and fear the Lamanites, even though their
fathers were once brothers with her ancestors. She remembered asking about that one time, and Cumeni's sharp and
angry reply. Now, thought Mara, despite his hatred of the
Lamanites, he and the other priests have chosen daughters
of their foe to wed. She had not thought of this before, dwelling on it and all these things in her mind.

Deep in her thoughts, it took her a moment before she
became aware of approaching voices. Since she and Zeram
traveled alone, speaking only to one another, the sound
startled her and she leapt to her feet. Glancing about the
clearing, trying to think where to hide, she recognized one of
the voices as his. What others dwelt or traveled in this wilderness? she wondered. Could Zeram have been taken captive by Nephite soldiers, or had he found other Lamanite
warriors? Her mind full of questions, she wondered if she
should flee, when Zeram stepped into the small clearing.

Mara's eyes went to Zeram's face, searching for some clue
to the strangers who accompanied him. At her questioning look,
Zeram smiled at her, his features transformed with a new happiness she had never seen in his face. She wondered who these
people were, the comely Lamanite woman, with black hair and
dark eyes, and the young man who appeared to be a Nephite
like herself. She wondered that Zeram held the woman's hand!

"Zeram?" Mara asked uncertainly.

He brought the young woman to Mara and said,
"Mara, my joy is very full. This is Saphira, my sister whom
I have sought all this time."

Mara didn't know what to think, amazed at such happenings. She wondered at the chance that had allowed Zeram
to find his sister, who now approached Mara, smiling.

"Zeram," Saphira said, though she looked at Mara when she spoke. "You did not tell me that the Nephite maiden is beautiful."

"Nor did Zeram tell me that his sister is so lovely," Mara responded, her hand gentle on Saphira's arm in a touch of welcome. Then suddenly the two women were weeping, clinging to one another.

Zeram moved away, standing by the Nephite. He glanced at Samuel, bewildered.

"I think they have been in the wilderness too long, without the comfort of another woman," Samuel said in a low voice.

Zeram understood, yet still the sight made him uncomfortable. Saphira pulled away, forcing a smile through her tears and Mara shyly answered the smile, embarrassed by her weakness. The Lamanite maiden began to laugh, brushing at her tears and Mara caught the frailty of the moment and all that the actions stood for. She shook her head, laughing through her tears and wondering at the tumble of emotions she felt.

"I have not truly wept, till now," she whispered to Saphira.

"I have wept—once," Saphira admitted.

She caught Mara's hand, pulling her back to her brother and the other man. "Samuel, do you know this Nephite maiden?"

The two studied each other. "I do not know your name," he said slowly. "But you are familiar to me. Are you not the eldest daughter of Cumeni?"

"Yes," Mara answered, surprised. "But I do not know you."

"I am Samuel, son of Heshlon, a high priest of King Noah. My father followed the king on the day of the great battle when he deserted his people, and I followed my father." He spoke almost reluctantly, the shame in his voice obvious. Mara slowly sat down on a fallen tree, not looking at him as she asked, "The man who was my father followed the king," she said quietly. "I would know if Cumeni still lives."

"Your father still lives," Samuel responded in a similarly subdued manner.

Mara looked up at him, her face strained. "He is not my father. On the day he abandoned me and our people, he ceased to be my father. On that day I also ceased to be Kheronai, daughter of Cumeni. I called myself Mara, because my pain was bitter."

He sat down beside her, his voice low. "I understand this thing," he said at last. "These past years I have borne a terrible shame, knowing that I followed my father in his weakness. If I could go back, I would have stayed and fought with my people."

"Our city fell into captivity."

"Better captivity, or even death, to shame. This is the reason that Amulon and the other priests stole Saphira and the Lamanite maidens. They were ashamed to go back to our home."

"Where are your father and the others?"

"I do not know. When Saphira fled, I followed, and we have not seen them for many days now."

Saphira looked up at her brother, wondering at the conversation of the two Nephites. Zeram motioned her to follow him. Away from the other two, Saphira questioned her brother with her eyes.

"Mara grieves for her father, although she does not understand it," he said.

"Do you understand it, my brother?"

Zeram was thoughtful. "I know my own grief at losing you and believing I would never find you, and at continually fearing for your safety. Mara's grief is different. Mine was one that turned to joy upon finding you, yet Mara's will be even more bitter should she someday meet her father." He took her hand in his and smiled. "You are safe! That thought comes to me again and again. Tell me all that happened to you, Sister. I want to hear all your words."

The sky glowed with burning embers, another day fading into night. Zeram stirred the fire with a stick, burning ash the color of the sunset billowing up. He tossed on part of a fallen log, then sat down against a large rock, holding a piece of bark filled with meat.

"Now tell us again, Zeram, how you came to meet at the sacred waters," Saphira asked, biting into the meat and roasted sweet root. "And how you already knew of Mara."

"We met first in battle," he said.

At Samuel's surprise, Mara nodded. Saphira, however, was disappointed at this brief telling. She knew the story from her days in the village, and felt much pleasure at meeting the maiden her brother had spared.

"She and the other maidens came to the front of the battle," Saphira said. "Because of this my brother and the other warriors stopped the war. At least that is the story told in our village," she added, a little embarrassed.

"And Mara has proved to be my most difficult adversary yet," Zeram murmured.

Mara smiled and bent her head, tasting the savory meat. Samuel looked at her. "Was it the same war our king fled from?"

"Yes," she answered. "When he and the priests left us, and our soldiers were dying in battle, the Nephite daughters were sent before our enemy to plead for mercy."

"The maidens went into the battle and bowed down before the warriors. It took much courage," Saphira added.

"Mara led them," Zeram said in a voice of quiet pride. "She came and knelt before me, and the other maidens did likewise. We could not help but feel compassion on the daughters of our enemy." His eyes went to Mara.

"This is why the city was taken captive, and not destroyed, then," Samuel said thoughtfully. He looked at the Nephite maiden. "You have much courage."

Mara pulled her head covering about her. "I did that which was necessary."

"But why have you since fled your home and come into the wilderness?" Saphira asked.

"I am looking for a man and his people who left our city some time before the war. Perhaps you knew of him," she said, looking at Samuel. "His name is Alma."

"Alma! Why would you want to find a man whose crimes made the king seek his death?"

His answer disconcerted Mara. "What were his crimes?"

"He sought to lead the people in rebellion against the king."

Mara thought Samuel was merely echoing the words he had heard the priests speak and she laughed shortly. "Ah, I see! Rebellion against the king who later abandoned his people to die at the hands of their foe?"

Samuel thought this over. "Perhaps I spoke too quickly. A rebellion against the king might have saved our city from captivity."

At his earlier words, Mara had felt impatient with Samuel, but now her countenance softened. "From what I have been taught Alma did not lead the people to turn against the king, but instead to turn to God. He taught the people of Christ, and they gathered to hear him. King Noah feared this and sought his life, and for this reason he fled the city."

"Where is Alma?" he asked.

Mara and Zeram looked at each other and she sighed. "I believe he is north from here, but I grow more uncertain each day."

"Mara, did you not say we would find that which we sought?" Zeram gently reminded. "Even this day have I not found Saphira?"

She smiled, her heart feeling lighter. "Yes, this is so, and I share your joy."

The four finished eating, each wondering at how their lives would now change and what direction they would take. Zeram had found Saphira, and now that Samuel knew the city of Nephi still stood he could return, or try and go back to his father and the priests. Or, if he chose to travel with Mara to find the people of Alma, then Zeram would be free of his obligation and could return home with Saphira. Yet as each pondered the possibilities, the logical answers were not the ones desired.

Mara finally spoke. "What will you choose to do now, Samuel?"

He didn't immediately answer, his eyes on Saphira. "I am not sure," he said at last.

"You would be welcomed in my search for Alma and his people, who would have much to offer. For certainly they do not live in captivity, and my teacher often told that they taught their doctrines to all who would listen."

Mara knew that in offering this choice to Samuel she would free Zeram to return home. And even as she spoke a great sadness filled her heart, forcing her for the first time to admit that she might never see Zeram again. She felt a quiet wonder that he who once was her enemy had come to be her cherished friend. Yet how could she ask him to stay with her, now that he had found Saphira? He had every right to take his sister and return home, Lamanite with Lamanite, Nephite with Nephite. Why did the old ways always win, kin against kin, brothers in hatred?

Saphira spoke to her kinsman. "Why have you traveled with Mara beyond the waters you spoke of?"

"I told her I would help her find what she sought, since she delayed her journey by tending me after the boar's attack," he answered, leaning forward to toss more bark onto the fire. "I also did not know where else to search for you."

"Did you promise to help Mara find these people?" she asked.

"It seemed a promise," he said after a moment.

"You must not break your vow, then. Mara will seek her people and you will fill your promise. We will go with you, and perhaps Samuel will seek to join them. Is this not the best way, my brother?" Saphira questioned, her voice threaded with emotion because she felt that she and Samuel were to be parted.

"Should I defer to the counsel of a mere woman?" Zeram said aloud.

"Perhaps it is wise counsel," Samuel stated after a while.

The four looked at one another, each feeling the tension at play. Mara knew she should speak, and free Zeram from his vow, but she did not. Instead she struggled with the feelings that kept her silent. Zeram felt almost angry as he faced the decision, knowing what any other of his kinsmen would do, yet unable to follow through.

"What would you have me do, Mara?" he finally said. "I have received counsel from one woman, I might as well listen to another."

Mara looked at him in surprise. Why did he ask her thoughts? At last she spoke. "You have found that which you sought."

He felt his heart grow heavy, realizing he had set his own trap. "It is so."

"You have every right to travel to your home with Saphira, and I will not bind you to your vow. But if I could chose, it would be to have you travel with me. Surely Alma and his followers cannot be so far away."

Quietly Mara grabbed the glyph, pulling it from around her neck. She studied it for a moment before handing it to the others. "This is the symbol that led me to cross the mountains, and gives me hope that we will soon find Alma's people."

She waited expectantly for them to understand. The tiny glyph had for so long now held her only hope, yet their reaction was not what she had expected.

Saphira and Samuel's expressions were blank, even as Zeram's countenance darkened. He let out an angry snort. "This?" he asked derisively. "This is what you seek? I know this symbol."

"How can you know it?" Mara asked, amazed.

"It is evil," Zeram angrily said. "And stands for everything my people have come to hate! It is a symbol used long ago by the Nephite religion to usurp the power of our throne. It was used to trick us, to deceive us so that your people might flee from us into the wilderness. I know the old stories."

"That is not true," Mara said, feeling hurt as he tossed it back to her. She wanted to explain his accusations away, but didn't know enough about Alma's teachings to do so. Quietly she slid the silk cord over her neck and let the glyph drop inside her tunic. What did this mean now? Would Zeram refuse to go with her?

Saphira spoke at last. "Will you tell us your decision, my brother?"

Zeram's dark eyes studied Mara in the fading light.

"A Lamanite does not break his vow," he said at last. "I have sworn to help Mara find her people, and I will not desert her."

Mara pushed aside her hurt feelings and managed a smile, her voice low. "I hoped you would not."

Saphira looked at the two men. "If I go with you, what of Samuel?"

Zeram leaned back against the large boulder, motioning to the Nephite. "I owe you a great debt, Samuel. We would ask you to join us, unless you seek to return to your father, or the Nephite city."

Samuel soberly thought over all he had heard, aware that Saphira's eyes impatiently studied him. "Perhaps these people would have something to offer," he said at last, wishing to ignore Zeram's accusations. "What is their doctrine?"

"They teach of God," Mara answered. "They teach of peace, and I was told their words are for all, bond and free, male and female. . . ."

Another time Zeram had scoffed at her words, but now he wore no expression so she took in a deep breath. "Even Nephite and Lamanite."

The others looked at her, pondering the thought. "Then I will go with you," Samuel replied.

"It is good, then," Saphira said, covering her smile and taking Mara's hand. "I would meet such a people who believe thus. Is such a place not full of promise, my brother?"

Zeram's dark eyes silently studied the two women before him. He thought of the glyph and did not answer.

CHAPTER ELEVEN

Zeram ran the honed edge of the stone along a piece of wood, shaping and fashioning the bow. Over and over he repeated the movement, shaving off thin slices of the wood to form the long, flat shaft. Saphira came over and sat down, watching him work. Her hair had been washed and plated, and the tunic she wore was Mara's extra one made of sturdy white linen. Her own of scarlet silk was in shreds, so Mara offered her the other tunic. Zeram thought his sister beautiful, her face clean and glowing, her eyes deep in thought. It did not surprise him that the Nephite man often looked at her with tenderness.

Across the clearing Samuel sat talking with Mara, intent on asking her about the people of Alma. Zeram felt uncertain in their presence now, again reminded of how different their two tribes were. He spent his attention on the bow, not looking at Mara. Saphira watched her brother in silence for some time before speaking.

"Samuel is much interested in these people we search for. What do you think of them?"

Zeram kept his eyes on the work. "I think they are Nephites," he answered at last.

"Even as Mara and Samuel are Nephites?"

He lifted the bow, running his hand down its length. "Mara and Samuel are different. You forget that I have gone into the Nephite lands many times, while you never left the land of Shemlon before. Often I have seen the deceit of their kind. Can you so easily forget the men who stole you and the others?"

"I will never forget," Saphira said in a sober voice. Zeram looked up at her, then laid the piece of wood across his knee.

"We have both seen much good in Samuel and Mara, but that does not mean their people are like them."

"I saw the cruel and cunning ways of the Nephite priests, yet Samuel showed me kindness. And Mara tended you when another might have fled. If there are two with mercy, then could there not be more?"

"I have seen no others," he stated.

"Not in the city Mara has left, even she herself spoke of the hardness of her people there. But what of these followers of God that Mara seeks? Could their hearts not be good, even as Mara's?"

Zeram smiled at her, his glance speaking of the patience he felt with her innocence. "It will not matter what doctrines they follow. They will be Nephites, and we will be Lamanites, their hated enemy."

"You could be wrong," she said, scowling at his stubbornness.

He picked up the bow, bending it across his leg to test for spring, then binding the cord to one end. "I am not wrong, Saphira."

"Then what will happen when we find the Nephites? Will we part with Mara and Samuel?" Her voice sounded tense, taut like the bow string he tied and stretched against the wood.

Zeram did not answer, instead he looked over at Mara, watching the way she sat in earnest discussion with Samuel, the way she brushed back the hair from her face. He pulled the string too tight and it snapped, the wood of the bow flipping back. In anger he set it aside and arose. Saphira came and stood beside him, resting her hand on his shoulder.

"What of Mara?" she asked, her voice low. "Will you leave her with the Nephites and return to Shemlon, never to see her again?"

His expression was one of stone, his eyes hard. "What of Samuel?" he asked in return, his own words slicing back at her. "He will seek his kind. Will you follow?"

Saphira bent her head, the single movement showing all the fear and uncertainty she felt. "I would not chose to be parted from you, my brother," she whispered.

The quiet avowal touched him and he reached up, placing his hand on hers where it rested on his shoulder. "There will be no other way," he replied, his own voice unhappy. "Do not go with him to the Nephites," he quietly said.

"Mara will go," she whispered. "And what then, my brother? For I know that the Nephite maiden has taken your heart."

If her words startled him he didn't show it, instead his face displayed none of his feelings. "If you go, I will lose you both," he said at last.

Then he pulled away from her, turning and walking into the deep of the forest.

When night turned the sky to black silk and gray clouds drifted across the expanse, Saphira sat on the low limb of a tree, looking up at the moody display overhead. She heard footsteps and turned to see Samuel approaching. She smiled at him and he straddled the branch, facing her.

"This is a pleasant place," he stated.

"Yes, I have been watching the night sky."

Their words drifted away, each aware of the other and the many unspoken things between them.

"Saphira?" His voice seemed tense.

"What is it?"

"I would speak to you about the things that have happened." He stopped, uncertain, but she motioned to him to continue. "I see much joy in you, now that you have found your brother."

"Yes, and I found him because you kept your word in returning me to my kin."

Samuel thoughtfully caught a small branch in his hands, his posture tense. "Would you despise me if I told you that I did not care if we ever found your kinsman? I am ashamed to say this, but it is true."

"Why would you wish such a thing, Samuel?" she asked.

He didn't immediately answer, instead struggling with the words. "Because now I will lose you," he said at last. "Your brother will take you back to your people, and you will be given to another as wife."

Saphira studied the shadowed line of his features. "This grieves you," she hesitantly stated.

"Yes," he answered in a low voice. "Such a thing would cut into my heart."

She reached out, touching his face with her fingers. He suddenly caught her hand in his and pressed his mouth against her palm. "Saphira, what will become of me when you are gone? My life was nothing before, only a hollow reed caught in the wind. And then I saw you, saw another hurt you and my blood turned to fire. I fought for you, and now having been with you all this time I would fight again. But how shall I fight against your brother, when you love him?" The anguish of his words made him move from the branch, standing stiffly with his back turned to her.

Saphira left the tree, coming to stand behind him. "He is not the only man I love," she murmured in a low voice. "There is another I have come to love, and not as a brother."

Samuel turned to face her, peering at her in the shadowed darkness. She moved into his arms, looking up at him as he bent his head. He kissed her, and held her to him, his hands stroking her hair. Then he kissed her brow and face. "Do not leave me," he said at last. "Do not return to your people, and leave me desolate without you."

"I will not leave you. I owe you my life." Her fingers touched his face.

"What of your people, and of mine?" he asked.

"I no longer care," she said, her voice filled with emotion. "If there is no place among my kind for you, and none for me amid yours, then it matters not. I will be with you, Samuel, for even a desolate place would be a haven if we were together."

He kissed her again. "What of your brother?"

Saphira smiled up at the man she had come to love. "We have one hope, and that is Mara."

Samuel thoughtfully stroked her brow with his lips. "If his heart longs for her as mine for you, then there is hope."

She laughed, the sound delighting him. "Despair not, for I believe there is hope."

He smiled down at her, then bent his head, burying his face in her hair.

The city stood like a deceptive vision glimpsed through the forest mists, and Samuel and Zeram lay on the incline, staring at the unique scene before them. In the far distance the edge of city towers and outer wall merged back into the mountain, and they couldn't determine where the city ended and the mountain began.

The jagged gray stone jutted skyward, and from that mountain a fall of water split the cliff, disappearing behind the city then flowing in a shallow river from beneath the city wall. The towers had been built from the mountain stone, making it appear to blend in to the sheer cliffs in such a manner that they had nearly passed it by. Below them the land broke free from the jungle, spreading out in a pleasant valley with trees that lifted shimmering leaves skyward. It was a place of pure water, and in the rising morning mist it appeared strange and beautiful.

"I have seen nothing like this before," Zeram said hesitantly.

"Neither have I," Samuel answered.

The two men looked at the scene in quiet until Zeram spoke again. "Do you think these are the people of Alma?"

Samuel moved away from the edge and sat up, and Zeram did the same. "I do not know, but I think it might be. Still, how do we find out? I cannot see simply walking down to the outer wall and asking entry. They would take us to be spies, and if this should happen to be Lamanite land, they might chose to put me to death."

"And if it is a Nephite city?"

Samuel smiled. "Nephite or Lamanite, it will not go well for one of us."

"Then we need to move closer to the city by night and keep watch, so that we can decide who dwells there."

Samuel thought this over and made the sign of agreement. "Good. Now let us hurry back to the women."

They stood and moved through the forest, each silently thinking about their discovery and how it threatened them. When they entered the spot by the shallow stream where the women stayed, Saphira could tell something had happened by Samuel's anxious expression.

She questioned them with her eyes. "We have found a city," Samuel stated.

Mara turned to Zeram. "A city! Where is it?"

"Beyond the edge of the forest."

"Is it the city of Alma?" she asked excitedly.

"We could not tell," Samuel said. "It is strange and beautiful in a land of pure water, not far from here. But it is also unlike any place we have seen before. It would be best to use caution in going there."

"Take me to see this place," she asked Zeram.

"No, Mara. It would not be safe. When night falls we will move in closer."

"I want to see it," she said stubbornly. "Samuel, will you take me? I only want to glimpse it and then return."

He glanced at Zeram. "We would have to use much stealth in going there."

"If it is the people of Alma there would be no harm to us."

"And if it is not?"

She looked at him exasperated, and he sighed. "I will take you to see, and then we will return."

Something in Zeram made him want to stop them, but he said nothing, watching the two slip into the forest. After a few moments he glanced up at Saphira, who appeared troubled. He sensed that she didn't share Mara's excitement. "If these are the people Mara seeks, what will happen?" she asked.

"I do not know," Zeram answered, uncertainty in his voice.

Saphira's words were suddenly cut off by a scream that rent the air. Zeram grabbed his spear, running into the forest. He leapt over a fallen log and splashed through a stream, his heart pounding. Fear quelled up in him, and though he had only heard the scream once it echoed again and again in his mind.

He burst through the trees, halting at what he saw. Mara and Samuel stood surrounded by men armed with lances and bows. He stopped, gasping for breath, his spear ready. And yet his heart fell, knowing they were many and he was one. He assessed the men. They were the foe, Nephites like Samuel and Mara. He could see the uncertainty in their eyes, wondering at the man and woman they found, and at the Lamanite that now faced them. Still, despite their arms they didn't move to take him and he stepped back.

"Throw down your weapons," their leader said. "And we will not harm you."

Mara's heart raced within her, fear for Zeram's safety greater than fear for herself. The immediate threat to his life combined with the knowledge that he might turn and flee, leaving her forever. Her mind silently cried out to him as she stood staring at the scene, her eyes pleading with both Zeram and her captors.

Zeram glanced at the Nephite, not believing the warrior's promise. He drew his long knife, yet at that very moment Saphira darted through the trees, halting at a place halfway between himself and the Nephites.

"Get back!" he cried, a new fear assaulting him.

Saphira stood, a bird poised for flight, caught between two winds. Her eyes went to her brother, her mind racing to meet the decision. If she went with Zeram they would flee from the Nephites, returning again to the land of Shemlon. She turned to Samuel whose eyes pleaded with her, begging as a desperate man begs for life. Her breath caught in her throat and she glanced back at Zeram, a silent look pleading forgiveness for an act not yet taken. With a cry she flew into Samuel's arms and he held her to him, his head bent over hers.

Mara stared at Zeram, tears suddenly shining in her eyes, her gaze speaking a thousand silent pleas. He stared at the two women that had surrendered to his enemy and with a groan threw down his knife and spear, the Nephite soldiers bolting forward to grab up his weapons and take him prisoner.

The sun reached its zenith when they stood at the place where the jungle overlooked the open vale and mountain cliffs. The growing warmth had caused the mists to fade so when Zeram and Samuel again saw the small city it shimmered in distant splendor. Mara caught her breath at the sight, her heart soaring with hope. She felt certain that this was the place they sought, even if her companions appeared worried.

"Is this the city of Alma?" Mara finally asked the leader.

The man glanced at one of the others near him and she could tell her words seemed to surprise him. Still he didn't look at her, or answer. Then she realized her forward gesture, remembering the ways of her people and that it was not a woman's place to ask questions. Mara lowered her head, wondering at how freely she had come to speak with both Zeram and Samuel.

They began their descent into the vale and Samuel spoke, repeating Mara's question. "Is this the city of Alma?"

One of the men glanced at him, his look guarded. "No, it is the city of Helam."*

The words hit Mara, a shock bringing her to sudden awareness of their situation. Her heart felt like a stone tossed into a pool, the hope of a moment before sinking beyond reach. All this time they had searched for Alma and his followers, and now they had come to a place unknown! Though the men appeared to be Nephites, were they of a group different from her own kind? She began to feel fear, more for Zeram and Saphira than even herself, for certainly these Nephites would not view the arrival of their enemy's children with ease.

Slowing her pace she moved back to Zeram's side, looking up at his grim countenance. He didn't look down at her, instead his eyes stared straight ahead at the city of his foe. Silently Mara slid her hand in his, feeling the warmth of his grasp as his fingers tightened around hers.

* Mosiah 23:2-5; 16-20

CHAPTER TWELVE

Zeram paced the room like a trapped lion, his muscles tense. His hands felt empty with no sword or weapon to defend himself, even though there was nothing of immediate threat to him. He glanced at the stone walls and high, arched windows that looked across the city. In anger he strode to one of the open arches, then with a groan of frustration sat down on the ledge. Far below he could see people working, many laboring at building parts of this new city. Others tended crops and herds kept within the high wall. The city was alive with activity, and the sounds of laughter and song often floated up to him. His view spanned the entire city, and yet he could see no common marketplace where wares were sold or bartered. Although the people appeared industrious he often saw men stop along their way to talk, while others gathered in groups, listening to teachers. Women with babies on their hips stood at the wells and talked, while small children played in the open courtyard by the water causeway or sang chants taught by their elders.

In the high place of the city stood the Nephite temple, and he could often see people taking sacrifice to the altar there. Looking high beyond the city he caught sight of the majestic cliffs, the waterfall making an impressive descent behind the outer wall. He had viewed the spectacle often, and his eyes still followed the same line that lifted upwards.

Silently he admitted that he had never seen such a place with its wide causeways and open buildings. Even the room in which he was kept bore great refinement. He glanced at

the pallet filled with feathers, the table and stools of polished wood, the woven hangings. The high ceiling and arched
windows were set to catch the morning and evening breeze
and kept the room from feeling like the prison it was. Zeram
didn't want for any item, either. A wooden platter sat on the
table filled with a variety of fruits and grains, some of which
he hadn't enjoyed for many a season. Meat and cheese were
also provided, and ewers of water for washing.

For two days he had wanted for nothing, even being gifted
with clothing. He now wore the longer breech skirt of the
Nephites, and a girdle of kid's leather. The garments suited his
needs, still he felt awkward without his knife tucked into the
sash. His captors had even brought new foot coverings, but he
wouldn't wear them. He had no need, caged in this room.

Several times a day a young man arrived to deliver food
and to see to Zeram's wants, while two armed men waited
outside. At first he assumed the youth was a servant, but his
open face and curious gaze were not the way of a slave. Yet if
the lad wasn't a slave, then how was he persuaded to serve
Zeram? The Lamanite rested his fists against the window's
arch, his body tense with frustration. He was a prisoner in
this tower, and yet treated with respect. The very puzzlement
of the situation gnawed at him. Were he cast into a dungeon
he would have understood, and been able to face his captors
with true hatred and courage. Yet they made his prison soft,
and he felt it must be a trap.

He again turned his gaze to the city, thinking of the others.
What of Saphira? He feared for her, even as he felt anger. Why
had she fled to Samuel, giving himself no recourse but to surrender? It wasn't in Zeram to understand the whims of a woman,
and his anger would have been great were it not for Mara.

His thoughts dwelt on her continually, for until now he
hadn't been apart from her in many days. He wondered if he

would see her once more before their foe dealt him his fate, or would her beauty attract the attention of the Nephites? Even now she might be given to another as wife. Such a thought filled him with angry misery. Last of all he thought of the Nephite Samuel. If Saphira bore like feelings for him, then Zeram understood why she had chosen to flee to his side.

Zeram's thoughts were disrupted by the sound of footsteps and he stood, his eyes on the door. He heard the heavy bar being lifted away and then the portal was pulled open. Instead of the young man three others faced him, all bearing sheathed weapons. One was the warrior who had challenged him to throw down his lance and knife. He faced Zeram.

"Will you come with us?"

The request surprised Zeram but he showed no sign except to move to the door. They lead him down the circular stairwell and out into the open courtyard. Zeram glanced across the wide spaces bright with afternoon light, his eyes scanning the city whose plan he had memorized from his tower view. He believed he could overpower his captors, or at least flee from them and escape the city. But he knew it wasn't his lack of weapons that kept him prisoner, instead it was his lack of knowledge about Saphira and Mara.

The Nephites lead him across the courtyard, through a high archway, and into a building. Inside was a fountain and pool, and tall wooden pillars supporting a high ceiling. Steps lead up to a place where a leader might speak or govern, but it was unoccupied. He heard running footsteps, his name called, and Zeram turned to the sound. Saphira ran towards him and into his embrace. He held her, thirsting for the comfort of one he loved.

"Are you well, my brother?"

Zeram stepped back and studied his sister, amazed by her appearance. She wore a tunic of fine white silk, girded about with a chain of silver. On her wrists were silver bracelets and her hair was plaited with colored threads. "I am well," he replied at last.

"Do you bear much anger at me?" she whispered, knowing it was her actions in turning to Samuel that had caused Zeram to surrender.

"Why did you do such a thing, Saphira?" he asked.

She glanced at the Nephite men, only willing to answer him privily. "Have you seen Samuel?" she asked instead. Then understanding from his expression that he hadn't, she felt disheartened. "I had hoped he was with you."

"I have been a lone prisoner in a tower. What of Mara?"

"I am here," a soft voice answered behind him.

Zeram turned to find Mara approaching him. His hands felt heavy by his side, longing to reach out and take her arms in his grasp. Instead he stood still, unable to hide his expression of concern. Mara looked more beautiful than he had ever remembered seeing her. She wore a simple tunic of dark green silk and a colored, fringed shawl tied across her hips. Her hair was caught back from her face with a carved gold circlet and hooped earrings brushed against her cheeks. Her appearance did nothing to reassure him, for had Mara and Saphira been clothed as he had last seen them he would not have so keenly felt the changes that were happening. He wondered what the Nephites planned for the two women.

Yet Mara's countenance seemed calm and she smiled at him. "Zeram, this is the place that we sought. These are the people of Alma."

Zeram felt little comfort in her words. "Are you a prisoner here, Mara?"

"No, and neither is Saphira."

"She is right," Saphira affirmed, moving beside Mara.

His look grew hard. "What Nephite man has bought you silks and gold?"

"That is not the way here," Mara answered, earnestly try-ing to reach beyond his hard exterior that left her feeling un-certain. She could sense anger in Zeram, and it constrained the joy she felt at seeing him. Although her heart was full from all she had learned, it was Zeram to whom her mind continually turned during the past two days. "This clothing was given us by other maidens, even as you have been given clothing."

"I have been a prisoner," he said, still aware of the sol-diers not far away.

The sound of approaching feet made Zeram look to the side, and he saw a man stepping near. The Nephite made it clear he had heard the words.

"We meant you no harm," he said, and Mara smiled a greeting.

"Zeram," she said, "This is Helam, for whom the city has been named.* He was a friend and teacher of Riplah's."

Zeram's quick glance let him take in the man's superior age. His hair and beard were white, although his face didn't appear old. He moved with ease, coming to face the taller Lamanite. "Mara has spoken much about you. She has told me of your mercy to the Nephite people, and to her. She also told of your courage in bringing her to our city."

"Is this why you have released me from the tower, and brought me here?" he answered stiffly, unaccustomed to such praise.

"Our men put you in the tower because there was no other place. We have no prisons in our city. Neither has it been our desire to lock you away, but we have been uncer-tain as to your presence here."

"Because I am your foe," Zeram said with full understanding.

There was silence for a moment. "How shall you be my foe, when we know nothing of one another?" Helam replied at last. "But foe or not, you are a mighty warrior and we dared not

* Mosiah 23:20

risk your escape. Samuel has told me of you, and that is why I have brought you here, in hopes that we may make a truce."

Saphira stepped near at the mention of Samuel's name, not daring to address the Nephite, still her posture was one of questioning. Helam looked at her and smiled. "Samuel is well, and anxiously waiting to see you."

"What will you do with us," Zeram asked.

"It is not for me to decide. I have come to take you to Alma, our leader. He would speak with you." He turned to the armed men. "Thank you for your aid, I will take them myself."

The soldiers left without question and Helam signaled the three to follow. They went across the building and through an arch, stepping into an open causeway. Zeram and the maidens followed as Helam pointed to the buildings.

"What do you think of our city?"

"I have seen nothing like it, not even those built by your people in the land of Nephi," Zeram answered honestly. "From the tower window I watched many toil, and yet I did not see a common marketplace."

"We have none here," Helam stated. "All things among us are common."

Zeram pondered this, marveling that such a way could work. When they passed by a place where a toolsmith sat making wares, he couldn't keep from speaking. "How shall that man live if he does not sell his tools?"

"He gives his tools to those who have need, even as others give him meat and clothing. There are no poor in our city. We have an abundance that all may share in."

"Then how shall you support your king?" he asked, struggling with the concept.

"We have no king."*

Zeram could hardly fathom such a thing. "Does your city govern itself?" he asked, amazed.

* Mosiah 23:7

"Each man governs himself and his family, in righteousness. There is very little strife here, and most is quickly resolved."

They walked on in silence and Mara looked over at Saphira, who smiled. "Zeram," his sister said in a low voice. "Did not Mara say this would be a place of peculiar teachings?"

Zeram didn't answer, his thoughts deep in pondering when they passed several people who signaled Helam in greeting. Some looked at Zeram with curious eyes, but most of the faces seemed open and friendly. Then they passed by the young man who had served him in the tower. He greeted Helam and Zeram, smiling as he went on his way.

"Is he a slave?" the Lamanite asked, unable to hide his curiosity.

This question stopped Helam who looked up at the warrior, his countenance serious. "There are no slaves in our city. Neither are there servants. To us the privilege of freedom stands above all else. The young man we greeted is Ahoran. He chose to serve you, and is no slave."

They continued on, nearing the edge of the city where the buildings gave way to fields. Mara looked up at Zeram, wondering about the calm happiness she felt at being in his presence. Her day and a half in the city had been filled with wonder and happiness at all she learned, and yet her heart had longed to see him again. Even now she pondered the stirrings within her at being in his presence again.

Helam lead them to a place on the outer edge of the city where men tended sheep. "Stay here," he said.

When he moved away Mara approached Zeram, placing her hand on his arm. "Helam is a man after the teachings of Riplah, and has spent many hours schooling me in their truths. My heart has found much peace here."

He looked down into her face and the uncertainty he felt began to ease. He didn't answer, instead speaking to his sister although his eyes remained on Mara's face. "What do you think of this place, Saphira?"

"These people are Nephites," she answered thoughtfully. "But they are not Nephites like those who took me from Shemlon. Instead they are much like Samuel. I have been shown nothing but kindness here."

Zeram thought over her words, not wanting to be swayed by what she spoke and yet wondering at what he saw. A man with a young boy at his side left the sheep, approaching them. He had a lamb in his hands that bleated weakly and sucked at his fingers. He greeted the three but didn't pass by. Instead he stopped and took a lambskin from under his arm, tying it on the lamb's back.

"Why do you do that?" Mara asked.

"Because this lamb's mother has died," he said, stroking the small animal's head. "And another ewe has lost one of her lambs. I have put its skin on this little one so that she will suckle it." He handed the lamb to the boy. "Take it back to the penned ewe," he said.

The boy took the lamb and hurried away, then the man turned to them. His face appeared kind, his movements calm. He bore no striking mien yet his eyes were powerful.

"Helam has told me of your coming," he stated, then moved to Mara. "You have had much faith in seeking us, my daughter. I know that Riplah is pleased you have honored his oath."

He took her hands in his, even as the realization of his words touched her. For a moment Mara could not under-stand what her heart told her, for she had envisioned him much older, or at least the age of her father.* His years were not great, still his eyes seemed to pierce her through.

"You are Alma?" she questioned, her voice quiet with wonder.

"I am."

* Mosiah 17:1-4

Mara didn't speak. She couldn't find words to tell how she felt at meeting him at last. Instead she stood facing him, her hands in his grasp. He smiled and said, "I knew Riplah well. He was a man of noble spirit. It is good that you have found us at last, Mara, and in time you will no longer call yourself bitter."

She didn't question how he knew so much of what was in her heart. "There has been much hurt," she whispered at last.

"And with that hurt you have gained courage. It will take another kind of courage, here, to let go of your pain."

She didn't speak at first, then managed to ask, "Will you teach me?"

"Our learning is for all who would accept it."

His words caused Mara to look at Zeram, and Alma let go of her hands, turning to the warrior. "I am Alma."

"I am Zeram."

"I have heard about you. Your arrival has brought much concern among our people," he said, yet his words didn't carry any threat. "Helam does not know what to do with you. Even now he and the others fear that you will escape and return to your people. There is much worry that you might lead other Lamanites here to destroy us."

"What will you do, then?" Zeram said, looking at the man that both disconcerted and intrigued him.

"What decision would you make, were I the stranger?"

Zeram didn't want to answer, yet he spoke the truth. "I would make the only possible choice. I would destroy my enemy."

Alma appeared thoughtful until he finally spoke. "But you are not my enemy."

Evening dusk twisted itself among the amber threads of late sunlight, a cool wind moving through the arches of the building. Pleasant strains of music floated on the air in the hall where Mara and the others sat, a feast having been placed before them. All about the chamber were furnishings of fine workmanship, yet the abode didn't speak of wealth as one might have expected in the home of the people's leader.

Saphira sat before Samuel, her heart full with the moment. They had spent the afternoon together and she no longer bore any fears or doubts. At the beginning of their journey they had talked of two peoples who were foes, yet Samuel assured her that in the city of Helam all dwelt in peace, and were of one heart. Here there were only the people of Alma, and all worked together. Saphira wore her happiness like a precious crown, apparent to all, most especially to her brother.

Yet despite Samuel's words Zeram felt unsure, wondering how the others could so easily fit in among these people while his own fate stood with great uncertainty. Instead he silently ate the food, his countenance sober.

"Will Alma join us?" Mara questioned.

"I do not know. He has many duties among his people," Samuel answered.

Saphira thoughtfully selected a piece of fruit. "I cannot comprehend why their leader works among the common people. Our king did nothing other than govern."

"Alma is their prophet, not their king," Samuel explained.

"And yet the people love him more than a king."

"This is so," he agreed.

"Life is much different here," Mara said. "The people are happy, and all things are shared among them.* Can there be so little strife with such wealth as they have here? My mind cannot understand the things which my eyes see."

* Mosiah 18:27

"Yet you are the one who sought this place," Saphira reminded.

"And now I understand why Riplah made me swear the oath to seek Alma and his followers. For in a place like this his teachings fall on fertile soil. There is much to be learned here."

The young boy who had been with the sheep entered the chamber and came to Zeram. "Alma wants to talk with you," he said.

Zeram stood, following the youth from the hall without glancing back. He went with the boy into a smaller chamber that looked out across the land. Alma was at the window, studying the city he and his people had built. He heard the other's tread and turned, waiting until the boy had left before addressing the Lamanite.

"I would speak with you, Zeram."

"You have decided my fate?" the warrior questioned.

"No," Alma answered. "I have no right to decide another man's life for him. I learned that lesson well when King Noah sought my own life. And have I not told you already that you are not my enemy?"

"Perhaps I am not your enemy, but still I am a threat to you. I am a Lamanite."

Alma was thoughtful. "You are not a threat in yourself, only that your warriors could take us captive. We do not seek war, and make few weapons. For this very reason we fled from our homeland. That is why Helam and the others have suggested we keep you here."

"How? Will you lock me in the tower?"

Alma laughed and made the sign of disavowal. "There is no place in this city that could keep you prisoner. You could have easily fled our walls. You only stayed here, in truth you only surrendered to our men at the very first, for the sake of your sister, and Mara."

Zeram wondered at the perception of the Nephite leader but said nothing. Alma continued. "Helam has thought I should ask you to take a vow, that you will stay with us."

Zeram thought this over, his voice quiet when he spoke. "No man can force me to take a vow."

"You are right. Neither will I ask a vow of you."

"If you will not kill or keep me prisoner, nor ask for a vow, what will you do?"

"I have decided upon a vow, but not as you think." Alma moved towards Zeram, placing one hand on his shoulder and sliding the other beneath his thigh. His face was close to the Lamanite's and he gazed into his eyes.

"Before the God of our fathers Abraham and Isaac and Jacob, I swear that no harm will befall you. And that in this city, and among our people, you will be one with us. I swear to honor you only as a friend, Zeram."

He released the Lamanite from his grasp and stepped back, seeing the bewilderment in the younger man's eyes. "You have my vow, now it will be your decision. We want you to stay as one of us, to make your home here. Yet if you feel to leave, it will be your choice. Our lives are in your hands, Zeram."

"You would trust me with the fate of your people?" he asked awkwardly.

Alma was thoughtful. "I trust in the God who made you, and I know of the man you are."

Zeram took in a slow breath, moving to the place where the chamber opened onto a wide ledge on the building's wall. He peered out over the city and at the shadows from the cliff which spread across the rooftops. "What will become of me if I stay?"

"We will teach you, even as we teach Mara and the others."

"I was a captain of war among my people. You have no need for such, here."

"We always have need of valiant men."

"When would you have my decision?"

"Zeram," Alma said, stepping near and resting his hand on the younger man's shoulder. "You owe me no decision. My vow was to you, so do what you will." He pulled his hand away, ready to leave, then stopped. "There is one thing more. Mara does not yet know how much she loves you. If you leave, you will not know, either."

The prophet silently left the chamber. Zeram stood still, watching the shadows deepen across the city, flickering lamplights setting soft spots of yellow in distant arches. Feelings of change and uncertainty stirred within him. He felt weak, only knowing the ways of war. The people here were different from everything he had ever known. They were not of his kind, yet neither did they have the ways of the Nephites he once despised. His mind turned to Mara, and Alma's last words resounded in his mind.

Mara stood before Alma, her hands in the comfort of his, even as his words filled her with uncertainty. "You have told him to leave?" she asked, the words barely breathed.

"No, my daughter. I have only told him that the choice is his."

Sudden emotions fought within Mara, frightening her with the fear of loss she felt. "Can you not keep him here until he learns what is offered? He has felt such anger at being a prisoner that he will flee before he can understand what is offered."

"Would you have me rob him of the very thing you sought?" Alma asked in surprise. "You greatly value your freedom, Mara. I believe you care too much for Zeram to ask this."

Mara lowered her head in shame, sudden tears stinging her eyes. She couldn't speak, her throat aching at the loss she so keenly anticipated.

"Go to him," he said at last. "Speak with Zeram now. If you do not, he will leave at sunrise and you will not see him again."

The prophet guided her into the hallway and then left. Mara stood alone, her soul aching. How had her once-enemy come to fill such a tender place within her heart, to bring her captive even as she sought her freedom? And how could she not have known until the very moment he would leave, that no matter how blessed her life would be in the city she would not be happy if Zeram were gone? She took in a trembling breath, determined to lift her face to him again, this time pleading another cause.

Zeram heard the soft tread and then felt her presence behind him. Mara stepped near, her hands encircling his arm. He looked down at her, down into the eyes of gentle brown that spoke with such emotion.

"Alma has told me he has given you freedom, that you may depart," she whispered, her voice heavy.

He turned to her, taking her face in his hands, his thumbs stroking her temples. "What would you have, Mara?" he answered quietly.

Sudden tears shone in her eyes. "I am weak," she whispered. "Will you despise me for the strength I lack? I cannot encourage you to seek your freedom, and return to your people. Were it my choice I would keep you prisoner, least you leave this place and I see you no more, forever."

The wetness spilled onto her face and his thumbs

smoothed it away. He bent his head, his mouth stroking the line of wetness. Then his lips touched hers, a gentle warmth that eased her sorrow.

"I have been your enemy," he murmured.

"You saved me from death with mercy," she said, moving into his arms. He held her close, his face buried in the sweet fragrance of her hair.

"Zeram, will you not claim the debt I owe? Will you not stay in peace among these people?"

He lifted his head, peering down at her, and the city behind her back. "Once you said that freedom was a greater thing than safety."

"I remember," she breathed. Mara reached up with her fingers, stroking his face. "And yet is not this deep caring between us a greater thing than freedom?"

He smiled, his eyes peering down into her very depths. "Who can deny words from such as yourself?"

"Will you stay?"

His countenance grew sober, deepening shadows etching the strong angles of his face. "Do you know what you ask?"

He didn't need to speak of the land and people he would abandon, or his trials at facing the task of learning this people's way of life. The difficulty of her request lay before them and Mara saw with sudden, painful clarity that the way would not be easy, even in this place.

"By asking you to stay I ask you to give up everything," she stated, realizing the full truth for the first time.

"Tell me to go," he pleaded.

"I cannot," she answered.

"Mara, I do not belong here among your kind. Will you return with me, to my people?"

The force of his question startled her and she stepped back, her hands still in his. "I would be despised among your kinsmen. Here you will be treated with honor, for even Alma speaks of you with praise. Here no man will despise us for the inheritance of our fathers."

He released her hands, letting her fingers slide through his. "How much shall I give, for this woman?" he asked in exasperation, trying to understand the emotions that roiled within him.

Mara looked at the Lamanite, her mind remembering another time. Slowly she knelt before Zeram, her arms open and palms upturned, her face lifted in pleading. "Will you not show mercy?" she asked, filled with emotion. "Will you answer my pleas, and not take away that which I have come to cherish?"

Zeram stared at her in amazement, then he reached down and caught hold of her, much as he had on that day so long ago. Yet now the maiden did not cry out, instead she came into his arms and he held her close.

"I will stay, and see if the words of your prophet are true," he answered at last. Mara looked up at him with great tenderness and the heaviness in her heart was replaced with joy. She laughed through her tears. "I can ask for nothing more."

She turned within his embrace, leaning her head back against his chest and peered out over the darkness that had settled across the land.

EPILOGUE

Still water filled the circular font that lay across the backs of twelve carved oxen, groups of three facing outward in each direction. Housed in a chamber within the temple, the font lay directly beneath an opening in the high ceiling.

According to Nephite custom, this building was patterned after King Solomon's temple. Alma, having helped King Noah plan the temple towers of the city of Nephi, brought with him this knowledge when he started his own city. The temple was built to align with the points where the sun rose and set at the equinox. The temple doors opened on these occasions so that the earliest rays of light, representing the glory of the Lord, could shine through. Today sunlight streamed into the baptismal chamber, shining off the polished heads of the oxen.

Zeram glanced over at Helam, the one who had brought Mara and himself to this place. The man's white hair and beard appeared in contrast to a face that didn't seem old. Zeram half wondered if the teacher of the Nephites had known that a pillar of morning light would stream through the opening at this very moment, piercing the water with color and turning Mara's hair to its most glorious hue. Certainly, at any other given time, light passing through the opening would slant and hit amiss on stone or wall. But at this precise hour it caught threads of dark gold in Mara's hair and touched her with lines of light.

The Nephite maiden stood at the edge of the font,

clothed in a tunic of white linen, her hair caught back with a circlet woven of gold wire. Her light brown eyes stared at the smooth surface of the water. She seemed to tremble slightly, as if the breeze through the open arch had power to sway her.

Zeram studied her. Mara had changed his life, his mind, all that he knew. In the beginning he had stayed in the city of Helam for her sake. Now, with the passing of seasons, he also stayed for his own reasons.

Mara met his gaze, and her heart felt tender. She walked over to him, and he rose, towering above her. She looked up into his face and seemed to read his thoughts. "You have come a great distance, my warrior."

A slow smile touched his lips. "Yes, my beloved. I started on my journey as a soldier who cared only for the battle, until the day I buried my sword in the earth instead of a maiden's heart. That act has forever changed me."

Mara laughed a little, a low, sweet sound, and her eyes never left his face. "It is hard to believe how afraid I was of you, because now I trust you with my life. You are not the only one who has journeyed far. We have both learned so much."

She thought of the hours they had sat listening to Helam and Alma, learning about the sacred teachings acquired from the prophet Abinadi. Mara also remembered when she and Zeram had sat in a small, square chamber beneath a beam of light filled with swirling dust motes. They had spent much time reading the ancient plates that told of the beginning history of their fathers. Zeram learned the truth of how the single ancestral tribe split into two, and some of the misconceptions of his fathers. This, more than anything else, helped him to expand his view. But even though he drank in their teachings about God and expanded the few Lamanite beliefs about the Great Spirit, it was Mara who leaped ahead.

Zeram's gaze strayed to the font. "It worries me, a little. . . ."

Mara understood. Zeram had more to learn, but she ached to be baptized now, so she could progress beyond this point. She leaned near, resting her hands against the broad expanse of his chest. "I am not going down the path without you, my love. I am only walking a little ways ahead."

He caught her face in his hands, brushing his lips against her brow. "I am coming after you as quickly as I can. There is still so much I need to know. I have so many questions, my mind thirsts for knowledge the way it once thirsted for war."

The sound of low voices disturbed the silence in the chamber, and Helam quietly greeted those who entered. Mara caught the silk cord from around her neck, slipping the neck-lace over her head. "Will you hold this?" she asked. Zeram looked down at the gold glyph that lay in his palm, suddenly flooded by the many remembered teachings of his fathers. He closed his fist, trying to push away the confusing feelings. Zeram followed after Mara who walked over to her new men-tor, Alma. With him were Saphira and Samuel, recently be-trothed. Mara looked at them all, a smile touching her lips.

"Mara, it is time," the prophet said.

"I am ready," she breathed.

Alma took her hand, leading her down the narrow steps into the font. They stood for a moment in the water, facing each other. "Soon I will baptize you, yet it must be with a new name, for the time has come to abandon your bitter sorrow. You must no longer be Mara, my daughter. Instead you will be Meorah, a woman of light."

Alma then turned her to the side, his right hand lifted heavenward. He spoke the words of the sacred baptismal rite, calling her by her new name. When his words ended he buried her beneath the water, then brought her forth in a shining spray. She opened her eyes, looking at Alma through rivulets of water, her heart filled with light. Her lungs nearly burst, not with lack of air, but because of the greatness she could not hold.

Alma led her out of the water where she stood dripping on the stones while Helam stepped forward, wrapping his cloak about her. She continued to look into the prophet's face.

"I understand," he said to her unspoken query. "It is the grace of God that fills your heart." Zeram stared at her radiant countenance. He saw the streaming light etching her in gold, and also felt the light which spread through her, reaching out to him. An intangible presence filled his being and surrounded him in a cloud of warmth. It was not a power he could reach out and grasp or one he could hear or see. But he felt it as surely as he felt the warm rays of an afternoon sun or the heat from a flickering fire. Slowly he opened his palm, looking down at the glyph of the tree. The teachings of his childhood once again fought against all he had come to learn.

"What about this?" Zeram asked, unable to hide the frustration he felt. "What about this symbol? To my people it has always represented the treachery so often done to us."

Alma moved near, looking down into Zeram's palm. He nodded solemnly, then looked up at the Lamanite. "Ah, the Lehi Tree. You misunderstand, my brother. This is the tree of Lehi's dream. It is what makes us brothers. You and I, and all our people, were once the united branches of this tree. We can be again, some day."

Zeram thought of all he had recently studied, of the teachings of the ancient fathers, and for the first time he began to understand what Alma's words implied. If Lehi was their common ancestor, then the tree of the vision was his heritage, too. He walked over to Mara, now renamed Meorah, who looked up at him with concern. It was dispelled as he carefully slipped the silken cord about her neck, letting the gold glyph lay against the damp cloth of her tunic.

"Do not hide this," he solemnly counseled.

She caught it up, studying it closely. "Riplah gave it to me. He said it had greater meaning than I knew."

"It was a gift from me to your grandfather," Alma said. "A symbol worn often by those who wish to come to Christ."

"This led me to you," she murmured. "I studied it often, yet until this moment I had not noticed the fruit. What significance does it have?"

Alma pulled the cloak more securely about her. "The fruit is a very important symbol revealed to our Father Lehi. For you see, Lehi's dream was much more than just a dream. He saw in vision God's merciful plan for his children. The tree represents his love for us.* Lehi saw the true meaning of this love in God sending his son. He saw that Jesus Christ, the Son of God, will come to earth and live among men as an example to them and then be crucified for the sins of the world. On the third day he will be resurrected and break the bands of death for us all." Alma's gaze lifted from the glyph and captured Zeram and Meorah's complete attention.

"The fruit is God's greatest gift, Eternal Life.† The Lehi Tree is reverently called the Tree of Life by the believers in Christ. It reminds us that we have been offered Eternal Life through God's love for us. But it is up to us to live so as to be worthy to partake of the fruit of the tree. It represents that which you have partaken of this very day. It is the reason you can abandon all bitterness to become a daughter of light. A woman who shines like a candle in the darkness. Lift up your heart, let your soul be filled with great cheer, Meorah."

"Meorah," she repeated with joy. As a follower of the Savior of mankind, she must let go of her doubts and fears. Someday she might, again, meet her father, Cumeni. But she would not be the vulnerable girl, Kheronai. Nor would she

*1Nephi 11:22, 25
†1 Nephi 15:36; D&C 14:7

be the young woman, Mara, whose soul was bitter. Instead she would stand before him, free of his painful legacy, because now she had become Meorah, a woman who would light the way for others.

Lifting her eyes she sought the three friends who gathered around her. As she reached her hand out to Zeram who neared, she sensed the change in him. "You were there at my most bitter hour when I became Mara. Now you are with me in my greatest joy as I become a woman of light," she stated.

"Meorah," he repeated slowly. "It is a very good name."

Zeram thought of a candle shimmering to disperse the darkness, to show the path ahead, and knew that she would continue to light his way.

About the Author

Katherine Myers lives in Boise, Idaho with her husband and four children where she is an interpreter for the hearing impaired. *The Lehi Tree* is her sixth novel. Previous LDS titles include *Joy in the Morning* and *Wind Against the Stone*. She is currently writing her next novel in *The Lehi Tree* series.